PRAISE FOR KRI

CW01431749

"Kristopher Triana writes beau[ ]
and intoxicating horrors, and h[ ]
characters, you get to know them [ ]
—**TIM LEBBON**, author of *The* [ ]

"Jesus! And I thought I was sick."
—**EDWARD LEE**, author of *The Bighead*

"There's no denying it. Triana is the Master of Extreme Horror!"
—**RONALD KELLY**, author of *Southern Fried & Horrified*

"Kristopher Triana is without question one of the very best of the new breed of horror writers."
—**BRYAN SMITH**, author of *Depraved*

"I'm blown away with what Triana can do and will read just about anything he puts out."
—**SCREAM MAGAZINE**

"One of the most exciting and disturbing voices in extreme horror in quite some time. His stuff hurts so good."
—**BRIAN KEENE**, author of *The Rising*

"Whatever style or mode Triana is writing in, the voice matches it unfailingly."
—**CEMETERY DANCE MAGAZINE**

"Triana is a master of affecting, distressing, and immensely powerful horror."
—**JONATHAN BUTCHER**, author of *What Good Girls Do*

"Kristopher Triana pens the most violent, depraved tales with the craft of a poet describing a sunset, only the sunset has been eviscerated, and dismembered, and it is screaming."
—**WRATH JAMES WHITE**, author of *The Resurrectionist*

BECAUSE YOU'RE MINE

KRISTOPHER TRIANA

BAD DREAM BOOKS

**FOR SIGNED KRISTOPHER TRIANA BOOKS AND
MERCHANDISE, VISIT: TRIANAHORROR.COM**

for the ladies

"The love song must be born into the realm of the irrational, the absurd, the distracted, the melancholic, the obsessive, the insane—for the love song is the noise of love itself and love is, of course, a form of madness."

—NICK CAVE

CHAPTER ONE

SHELBY INJECTED BLEACH INTO THE dialysis lines. Using a urine sample jar, she'd collected nearly a cup's worth in the janitor's closet, then snuck it onto her cart before heading to the treatment center. It was on the first floor of Merrimack Memorial Hospital, making it easier for the patients to access during their appointments. That they needed such special treatment—that they needed dialysis at all—was proof of their uselessness. These pathetic people were wastes of the nurses' time and the hospital's resources. Shelby believed if you needed your blood to be filtered, your time on Earth was up, and you should have the decency to go gracefully instead of being a burden on your loved ones, medical staff, and— frankly—society.

The patients under this treatment were all either mean grandpas who made inappropriate comments, or rat-faced

Karens who were impossible to please. They had nothing left to offer others. All they did was *take*, contributing nothing but complaints as finer physical specimens than themselves waited on them hand and foot.

Shelby was doing the rest of the world a favor. But that wasn't her motivation.

After poisoning the lines, she performed general maintenance on the machine and sterilized it, her skin tingling with an excitement she could not share. This was one of her private joys, like dancing alone or eating ice cream right out of the carton, only far more exhilarating. It'd been nearly two weeks since she'd injected Mrs. Gunther with heparin, triggering the internal bleeding that ultimately killed the woman. It'd been a deliberate, secret assault on a patient, and just like with the others, Shelby had gotten away with it.

But while the thrill of taking a life was incomparable, it was as short-lived as an orgasm. She could ride the afterglow for only so long before having to discard the resin for a fresh hit. Luckily, as a medical professional, she was always surrounded by potential victims who not only deserved to die but had also passed their expiration date.

Shelby wheeled her cart back to the elevator, her breath catching when she saw Dr. Santoni approaching. The fluttering in Shelby's chest made her itch to hit the CLOSE DOOR button or flee the elevator altogether, but her own cart cornered her. It would seem strange for her to run from the doctor. It wasn't like he knew Shelby had a crush on him—at least she hoped not. As he stepped inside, Dr. Santoni gave her a polite smile. The doors closed, isolating them.

"What floor?" he asked.

"Three, please," she managed.

As he hit 2 and 3, Shelby stared at Dr. Santoni's hand. It was hairy and much larger than hers, even though she'd gained weight in the past year.

Tall, dark, and handsome, she thought, admiring the broad shoulders beneath his white coat. Doctors always preached about the importance of exercise, but it was rare to see one this fit. At thirty-nine, he was a decade older than Shelby, but she didn't consider that a problem.

Men before boys, she thought, staring at his face in profile. The strong jawline. Green cougar's eyes behind his glasses. Thick, Italian hair. She imagined running her fingers through it, and that made her think of his chest. Judging by the backs of his hands, Shelby figured he had a luxurious carpet over those pectorals.

She'd searched for the doctor's social media accounts, hoping to find some beach vacation photos or other revealing shots, but the doctor kept his pages private, so Shelby could only see his profile picture—Dr. Santoni with an attractive redhead. The woman was clearly older than Shelby, but she felt the redhead was prettier, sexier, and thinner—definitely thinner.

Shelby cursed herself. She'd been so excited to hear about Dr. Santoni's divorce, but that was seven months ago, and she'd failed to make a move. Now he had someone else. It shouldn't have surprised her. Shelby didn't even know how to flirt with someone like him, as evidenced by the awkward silence she maintained during the elevator's slow ascent.

As the doctor exited, Shelby sighed, and the doors closed on her, just as so many other doors had. The elevator rose again, giving her a moment of contemplative solitude in which to hate herself before delivering her to the third floor. She was staring down another double shift. A national shortage of nurses was overworking Shelby and her colleagues, but it also meant she was more valuable, and therefore could get away with more.

She headed to the supply closet and opened it with her badge. The built-in pharmacy seemed to glow, the white bottles responding to the fluorescents like sperm under a black light. Checking her chart, she went down the list of medications she needed for her patients and loaded up. She then gathered some items on her mental checklist—goodies for her personal use.

Narcotics didn't appeal to Shelby. She wasn't interested in getting high off pharmaceuticals, and even if she were, she wouldn't get them from the hospital. People noticed when morphine, Dilaudid, or Adderall went missing. But insulin, digoxin, and potassium chloride had no street value and didn't offer a high. No one raised an eyebrow when medications like these disappeared. It was attributed to simple inventory errors if it went noticed at all.

Lining the vials in neat rows, Shelby exited the supply closet and wheeled down the hallway, smelling the urine and riboflavin in the stale air—the fetid breath of all medical centers. At five-foot-two, her chest just barely cleared the cart's handlebars. Her breasts had grown bigger in the past year—one of the few changes to her body she didn't resent. Unfortunately, they weren't her only parts to have expanded. She knew she was fixating on her weight, but that only made her feel more pathetic. *Either lose the weight or stop harping on it,* she thought, wishing she could follow her own advice. Whenever she complained about her thickness to her doctor, she only told Shelby she was a healthy weight and suffered from body dysmorphia, but Shelby didn't believe that. She stared at her hands as she pushed the cart. They'd swelled too, reminding her of latex gloves filled with water. Not fat, but *ballooning*, like the rest of her. Her gnawed fingernails weren't doing her any favors either.

Maybe get a manicure on your day off, she thought, teasing herself.

With the hospital being so short-staffed, she'd been working six days a week for the past twelve weeks, and often pulled double shifts. Days off were spent running errands and doing housework in her one-bedroom apartment. Racking up overtime was helping her pay down her debt, but her personal life, which had been microscopic to begin with, had rotted like a jack-o'-lantern in late November. And now, to add another pile of shit to this broken toilet, her thirtieth birthday was steadily approaching, and she had nothing planned.

No boyfriend, no family, and no real friends, she thought as she rolled on to the next wing. *Fat, scarred, and alone. Happy birthday, Shelby Brandt.*

As she reached the room of her first patient, Shelby wondered if she'd be murdering him today. Though she'd already poisoned a dialysis machine with bleach, she wasn't sure that would be enough for her. There was a chance it may not cause a fatality, only illness. Shelby sighed again. She was in such a foul mood—exhausted, lonely, and wrought with a self-pity that sickened her. Terminating Mr. Pinsent might cheer her up, even if he was on the express train to the morgue already, given his advanced age and myriad of health problems. A little bleach injected into his IV line should do it. A fitting end to a crusty old fart.

But when Shelby entered the room, the geezer was awake. He sat upright in the inclined bed, watching a soap opera. When he turned to her, the old man glowered, his wooly eyebrows reminding her of a Muppet.

"Damned TV is broken," he grumbled. "Why can't I find any entertainment for *men?*"

"It's daytime TV, Mr. Pinsent. It's all talk shows and soaps. Maybe we can find you a nice movie to—"

She went for the remote, but he snatched it away from her.

"Don't touch my stuff!" he said. "You nurses all have sticky fingers. All of ya!"

"Actually, the remote is the hospital's property."

The old man sneered, hairy nostrils flaring. "Don't sass me. I pay your salary. All I know is my personal belongings have disappeared and you—"

"Your daughter-in-law took your things home for you, Mr. Pinsent."

"—goddamned nurses keep coming in here—"

"To give you treatment."

"—bothering me when I'm sick with the diabetes, trying to steal from me—"

Shelby's lips peeled back from her teeth. The urge to snap at the curmudgeon was making her tremble, but she knew better than to get in a screaming match with a patient. She didn't want to draw the attention of her coworkers— particularly not *negative* attention. She'd been diligent about maintaining a façade of normalcy, presenting herself as a cheery young woman with a positive attitude and strong work ethic, a team player who lived to aid the sick and help others. Like a professional wrestler, she was forced to always stay in character. The costume was so far from her true self that she often dissociated, as if she were leaving her body so this phony, philanthropic spirit might possess it. It was a necessary inconvenience, as was everything that kept people from knowing the true Shelby Brandt.

Pinsent continued to gripe, but she managed to lean him forward and undo his gown so she could access his side. She swabbed his love handle with alcohol, then prepared the syringe. Pinsent's chart stated three units of insulin were all his doctor called for. A dose ten times that could easily cause the patient to suffer hypertension and bradycardia, but Shelby wanted to catapult Pinsent's miserable soul into the arms of the Grim Reaper, so she settled on giving him a dose a hundred times more powerful. At the very least, he could fall into a hypoglycemic coma, which would not only give Shelby a break from his rants but also supply her with the gratification of bringing someone to the brink of death only to have them—or *allow* them to—survive.

As she stuck the old man with the loaded needle, he whined like a child. "Be careful, will ya? Jesus, a *dog* has more grace than you people."

Slowly injecting, Shelby watched the insulin flow out of the syringe and into Pinsent's decrepit body. She smiled, savoring the moment, feeling better than she had all day. Already she was debating which shocked expression would be best when someone gave her the news of another lost patient.

Finishing up, she wheeled out of the room, ignoring Pinsent's complaints about the food and the temperature of the hospital. Soon these little things wouldn't bother him anymore. He'd be far more concerned with the molecular chain reaction eating his heart's muscle cells, but he would be too dizzy and confused by hypoglycemia to understand what was happening until he went into full cardiac arrest.

As a patient with a long history of heart problems, his sudden death by heart attack wouldn't even come as a surprise to his doctors and loved ones.

He would simply go into the ground where every old piece of shit belonged.

CHAPTER TWO

BRYAN RAN HIS FINGERTIPS ALONG the swell pedals, then grazed all sixty-one manual keys. Glimmering from the fresh cleaning, the organ almost looked new. One would never guess it had been in his family for almost five decades, first belonging to his Uncle Martin, who'd taught Bryan how to play. Martin had performed "Amazing Grace" on it at the in-home wake of Bryan's grandfather. After that, the organ was passed down to teenage Bryan, replacing his keyboard. He'd been playing it ever since—thirty-six years of mastering everything from Bach to Iron Butterfly.

The oak bench was cool enough to feel through the slacks of his Burberry suit. A chill went through Bryan's thighs, and he straightened his posture before returning his hands to the organ. He breathed deep of the combined aromas of wood polish and the cologne on his neck. Putting his toes against the foot pedals, a tingle went through Bryan's extremities, his fingers trembling with anticipation as they hovered over the manual keys, prepping for C minor. This would lead to a Tierce de Picardie, utilizing the full organ.

The fourth movement of Léon Boëllmann's *Suite Gothique* filled the manor house like a dark dream. Bryan always enjoyed how the piece sounded like the film score of a horror movie from the days before color. Something with Lon Chaney or Peter Lorre. It was the most well-known movement from the suite, but Bryan didn't mind its popularity. He believed the classics were classics for a reason.

The manor swelled with the music he produced. It was almost like a church at times like this, the only sound being the organ as Bryan came as close to spirituality as he was capable. His heels pumped as every finger danced. The hair on his hands rose in excitement, and visions of classic monsters ran amok through his mind—werewolves and vampires pillaging villages in a thirst for virgin blood. Steaming splatters burst through his imagination. Then the memories came, moist and stimulating. The gleam of a blade. Various shades of red. The screams of the helpless. Like the organ, it was hard to believe these memories were as old as they were.

Bryan wished he could doubt the concept of linear time. Those feverish days seemed like a lifetime ago, and yet he'd found it difficult to accept the anniversaries when they'd entered double digits. It made him feel like a geriatric sheep put out to pasture, even if he was the one who'd put himself there.

He didn't hear his mother calling until he'd finished the suite. Hopefully she hadn't been calling for him long. Mom was irritable enough without having her patience tested.

Bryan scooted off the bench and pushed it back in place, tapping it three times before leaving the den. Reaching the winding staircase, he hit the switch for the chandelier, using the dimmer dial to keep the glow to a muted bronze. It was his mother who demanded the curtains be open and every light in the manor always be on. Bryan didn't care that it was a waste of energy; he just preferred the comfort of darkness. He'd always been that way. Cold, rainy afternoons pleased him more than a cloudless summer day. Sunshine didn't appeal to him the way dead leaves and morning ice did. When he'd been young, Mom had often yelled at him about keeping the house "like a morgue." But these days, she couldn't leave her room enough to notice. Bryan considered it a minor blessing.

His mother shouted his name again.

"Coming, Mom," Bryan called up the stairs.

Like the organ bench, the banister was cool to the touch. Though he kept the drapes closed, he'd opened the windows to allow the October air to infiltrate the manse. The crisp breeze was nostalgic, reminding him of happier days and better nights. Reflections of his youth were always bittersweet, and lately they'd been occupying his thoughts more than ever. Now fifty-two years old, Bryan looked back on even his thirties with the same feeling of distance as he did his high school days. Those memories were so far from his current reality to seem like mere figments of an imagination tortured by silent despair.

"Bryan!" Mom shouted again as he walked down the hall. "Where the hell are you?"

Bryan cursed under his breath as he approached the door. It was always kept a quarter of the way open, allotting Mom privacy while also keeping Bryan on call. He tapped three times, pushed the door open, and stepped inside, the daylight hitting him like an assault. Bryan squinted and reached into the breast pocket of his suit for his sunglasses. Seeing them, his mother huffed.

"Don't be so melodramatic," she said.

"You know the light hurts my eyes."

"Oh, please. You don't know the first thing about pain. When you were born, you wanted to come out feet first. Experience *that* and maybe I'll let you tell me about pain."

Bryan rolled his eyes at the old story, knowing she couldn't see him do it behind the shades. His mother was as redundant as she was ornery, her bitter personality matching her grotesque appearance. Overweight, liver-spotted, and balding, the seventy-five-year-old woman was misery for the eyes, just as painful for Bryan to look at as the sun itself. While tidy, the room made Bryan nauseous too, with its golden bedsheets and antique yellow dresser. An assortment of prescription bottles covered the nightstand, with an asthma inhaler resting atop a bag of hard caramels.

"What is it?" Bryan asked. Better to get to the point so whatever this was could be over with. "What do you need?"

She grimaced. "I know, I know. Too busy to take care of your own mother."

"I'm right here, aren't I?"

"But I've been calling for you for half an hour. You just kept on playing the goddamned organ."

"I played a single movement that lasts just four minutes."

She sneered. "Are you going to help me or just contradict me?"

"Of course I'll help you. Now tell me what's wrong."

But judging by the smell in the room, Bryan could already guess. His mother looked away, too ashamed to say it, but pointed in the bedpan's direction. Bryan removed his suit jacket and rolled up his sleeves, put on latex gloves, and then retrieved the bedpan and dumped the mess in the adjacent bathroom's toilet. There was blood in her stool again. Bryan put the bedpan in the sink and returned to the room with wet wipes to begin the worst part of this. Once his mother's backside was clean, he applied the baby powder she liked and helped her roll onto her back again.

"You're a good boy," she said, patting his arm. "You just frustrate me, is all."

You're a bad mom, Bryan thought, *and you frustrate me beyond words.*

"Anything else I can do for you right now?" he asked.

The old woman sighed. "I keep seeing stink bugs. They're always crawling up the walls where I can't reach to smush them, but the moment you come in, they hide."

Yesterday it was ants. Today it was stink bugs. Tomorrow it could be spiders or flies or ladybugs. Insects were not only his mother's pet peeve but also one of her most durable delusions. She entertained many hallucinatory beliefs. To Mom, cell phones caused cancer and the banks couldn't be trusted, so she'd put thousands in cash inside the home safe. As if her physical ailments weren't challenging enough for Bryan to deal with, his mother's cognitive abilities were in rapid decline, and this was a mind that had never been stable to begin with.

"I'll buy more insecticide," Bryan said. "Anything else before I get back to practicing?"

"Practicing?" His mother smirked. "You can't call it *practicing* if there's never an actual performance. You haven't played before an audience since college."

Bryan's shoulders went tight. "Mom—"

"Your Uncle Martin spent all that time teaching you, and you've just squandered that gift. I should've sold that organ years ago."

"But it's *my* organ."

"Well, it's *my house*. That thing takes up too much space."

"Mom, for God's sake, we live in a mansion. There's plenty of—"

"I say that thing is an eyesore. And you play it too damn loud."

He didn't bother arguing further. Nothing was more excruciating than engaging his mother in conversation, and nothing was more futile than disagreeing with her. Her mind was closed tight, and she'd never allowed others to change it no matter how solid their argument. The last thing Bryan needed was another groundless lecture from the old crone about how he should use his skills as an organist. If he chose not to play for others, that was his decision, not hers.

"I'll try to play more quietly," he lied.

Mother grumbled but said no more. She stared out the window at the weeping willow tree. It had turned gold over the past few weeks. It made Bryan uneasy when his mother gazed upon it like that, but he reminded himself it was simply her favorite of all the trees on the estate's sixteen acres. She didn't know what secrets it held. Only Bryan knew why the willow wept, and that made it even more special.

Returning to the bathroom, Bryan started washing the bedpan, but his mother suddenly cried out. The shriek was piercing, causing his whole body to tense. The bedpan fell into the soapy water and Bryan rushed back to the master bedroom, where his mother lay sprawled across the bed, clutching her chest. Her face was pink with pain, eyes bulging, making her resemble the insects she hated. She tried to say his name but could only wheeze it out.

Seeing his mother in this vulnerable state made Bryan tingle. He had to stifle a grin every time she suffered like this. Luckily, his sunglasses concealed the glow in his eyes.

"Mom!" he said, acting concerned as he went to her side.

"Amm," she whimpered. "Amba . . . ambulamm . . ."

"I'll call for one right away!"

Bryan sprung toward the door and burst into the hallway, but once he was out of her sight, he descended the stairs at a leisurely pace, humming behind his smile. He knew he'd left his phone upstairs in the pocket of his blazer. Pretending to search for it gave him an excuse to stall, bettering the chances that the old hag would die before the paramedics arrived.

Bryan was overdressed for a hospital visit, but being a middle-aged man with sartorial style, he was always overdressed for everything. That he carried a cane with a sterling silver wolf's head for a handle made him even more debonair. It pained him that most men had lost all sense of fashion. Grown men in Captain America T-shirts and cargo shorts made Bryan cringe. He wished he'd been around in the 1940s when suits, trench coats, and fedoras were the standard.

Harsh fluorescent lights soiled the halls of Merrimack Memorial Hospital, hurting his eyes, but Bryan kept his sunglasses in his pocket so not to draw further attention to himself. At times like this, he could almost deign to wear a baseball cap, as the visor would block the light and conceal his eyes from others. He didn't want to see or be seen. Eye contact was how trouble began. He just wanted to get in the obligatory visit with Mom so he could return to the manor house. In her absence, it had become a serene sanctuary. Bryan hoped his mother would stay in the hospital for as long as possible. They could easily afford it. She'd never consent to any sort of assisted living community, but a prolonged hospital stay was a possibility that tickled him.

As he proceeded down the hallway, the open doors to patients' rooms gave him brief glimpses of medicinal misery. Though he disliked hospitals because they reminded him of his own mortality, Bryan was always more comfortable around the sick and the dying. Healthy people—*young* people especially—filled him with a quiet rage he'd worked too hard to subdue. Being surrounded by the crippled and diseased had a way of calming him and even inflated his self-worth.

At least I'm not them, he thought.

Reaching his mother's room—a private single she'd paid extra for—Bryan spotted a blond nurse bent over Mom's bed, administering something he couldn't see from the doorway. She was slender and young, maybe mid-twenties, and though he could only see her from the back, a quiver went through him. This was just the sort of girl he would have pursued as a young man. Now such girls were unobtainable. For this, he loathed her instantly.

She turned to face him, her pale green eyes magnified by her glasses. Her fair skin was flawless. Bryan imagined it would taste as pure as spring water upon his tongue. The nurse's attire left much to the imagination regarding her physical form. Bryan longed for the days when nurse uniforms were tight, white dresses with cute hats, before everything was ruined by these dumpy pajamas. It was just another painful reminder that the world he'd grown up in was gone.

"Good morning," he said.

"Actually, it's early afternoon," the nurse told him.

Bryan gripped the handle of his cane tighter, annoyed at being corrected when it was unnecessary. What difference did it make what time it was when he was just offering a polite greeting?

"I'm Bryan Vives. I'm her son."

His mother had her eyes closed, but Bryan wasn't sure if she was unconscious. If so, he'd have to wake her. She would never believe him if he told her he'd come by while she was asleep, and he wasn't about to make a second trip in a single day.

"How is she?" he asked.

"Better today," the nurse said in a flat, unenthusiastic tone. She continued whatever it was she was doing with the hoses and dials. "Heart rate is back to normal."

"On the phone, the doctor told me she's stable, but still wants to keep her for further tests."

The nurse scribbled on her clipboard. "Yes. Dr. Savalas wants to observe your mom a little longer."

Bryan gazed upon his mother's slack face. "How long?"

"You'll have to ask the doctor, but I'd guess just a few more days. Don't worry, you'll have her back soon."

"There's no rush. I mean, we want to make sure she's responding well to the new medications before she returns home. And I want every possible test performed. Spare no expense."

The nurse only nodded. Still looking at her clipboard, she didn't notice the twitching in Bryan's cheek. The handle of his cane had gone slick from his sweaty palm. Hospital rooms were always uncomfortably warm and stale, but this wasn't the cause of his perspiration. He didn't want his mom to come home yet, if at all. He also didn't want this little nurse bitch to enjoy another second of life without being in agonizing pain, but there were limits to the things he could control. Just staying in control of himself took an exhausting amount of effort. It's what motivated him to live reclusively, despite his loneliness.

"We're doing everything we can, sir," the nurse said, not hiding the annoyance in her tone. "Enjoy your visit."

Gathering her things, the nurse left the room without a goodbye, and Bryan turned his attention to the bloated juggernaut who'd spawned him. Mom usually snored like a Saint Bernard when she was asleep, but now she was as silent as a corpse. He preferred her this way—passed out with hoses up her nose and needles in her veins. It gave him hope she would someday die, that his fear of the hag hanging on forever was indeed irrational. It was a shame he had to wake her.

Bryan shook her shoulder. "Mom."

The old woman snorted but didn't stir.

"Mom. Wake up. It's Bryan."

But who else would it be?

There was no one else left to care about Beatrice Gibson-Vives. Her husband, Camilo Vives, was long dead, and they'd had no other children. Her parents and only sibling—Bryan's Uncle Martin—were also deceased, and she was estranged from her extended family. Bryan couldn't remember a time when he and his mother weren't the black sheep of the Gibson clan, a dark secret tucked away in the guest house all those decades. Now, with Uncle Martin gone, the family fortune Chet Gibson had gained over a lifetime of lucrative real estate ventures was bestowed upon his remaining descendants—his crackpot daughter and the grandson he'd never accepted. This was much to the chagrin of the extended family, who'd never liked or trusted Beatrice, objected to her marrying a Cuban immigrant, and subsequently resented Bryan's very existence.

The Gibson clan were xenophobic, New England blue bloods who didn't appreciate their family tree being blemished by a nonwhite baby. Even the community's Catholic church, which Beatrice had attended her entire life, had refused to perform the marriage ceremony because of Camilo's ethnicity. And so they'd eloped, which only further angered Beatrice's father. Bryan had dealt with the family's residual disdain all his life. That his grandfather's estate would soon fall to him, because of an overlooked technicality in the old man's will, gave Bryan considerable joy. Not just because the wealth enabled him to live comfortably without having to work, but also because he knew how it infuriated all those greedy Gibsons who'd never expected Chet's fortune to end up in the hands of the boy they'd ostracized.

"Wake up, Mom," Bryan said, shaking his mother harder.

If not for the monitor's steady beep, he could have mistaken her for dead. His mind buzzed with images of her blued corpse stretched out on a slab, naked and ice cold, her dead eyes staring into the morgue's harsh fluorescent lights—staring *through* them.

Bryan had seen that lifeless stare before, when the light behind the eyes of the living faded, dragging all that promise and all those dreams into the obsidian vortex that awaits us all. Sometimes the light went out in a sudden burst, like when a bulb burns out. Other times it was a slow dimming to that sweet, irreversible darkness as the heart stopped pumping and the brain ceased firing synapses. Sometimes the eyes closed on their own, just like in the movies. But most of the time, they stayed open—*staring*. That's why people once put pennies on the eyelids of the deceased, and why undertakers sowed the eyes of the dead shut before their open casket funerals. Most people didn't want to look into the eyes of the dead.

Most.

Bryan patted his mother's cheek three times. "Mom! I said *wake up*." He patted harder—*one, two, three*. "Mom. For Christ's sake."

Drawing his handkerchief, Bryan wiped the sweat from his brow, cursing under his breath. He wondered what would happen if he started yanking all her hoses out. Would she wake up? Would she experience a medical emergency?

Would she *die*?

Certainly the machines would alert the nurses. Bryan wouldn't want to have to explain himself.

"Fine," he said, grimacing. "But I was here. You hear me, you old battleaxe? I was *here* today, and I don't want any grief from you about it later."

He tapped his cane on the floor three times, as if he were striking a gavel, then turned on his heels to face the exit. Just beyond the doorway, another nurse was watching him from the hall. Her black hair was in a tight ponytail, and her eyes seemed too dark for her cherub face. She held Bryan's gaze. When he didn't blink, the nurse looked away and pushed her cart along. Bryan stepped into the doorway to watch her go, hoping she would turn back to look at him one more time, though he wasn't sure why. She was a curvy girl, and Bryan enjoyed the rearview as she disappeared around the corner without looking back.

She must have seen him shaking his unconscious mother, but she'd not scolded him for it. She hadn't even given him a dirty look. The girl had only watched until Bryan stopped putting on the show.

CHAPTER THREE

AFTER PLACING THE BAGS OF blood in the fridge, Shelby disposed of the syringe in the medical waste container. She'd used it on patient Mr. Williamson, drawing just enough of his blood to infect the clean blood in the transfusion bags. Mr. Williamson was hospitalized because his HIV had recently transformed into AIDS, and Shelby immediately seized upon this opportunity. While AIDS wasn't the death sentence it had once been, it remained a harrowing diagnosis and came with a terrible stigma. Shelby giggled, thinking of the emotional damage this would cause the unsuspecting victims who received one of these tainted transfusions. She might never see those patients again and they may never trace their infection back to the hospital, but it was satisfying just knowing she'd permanently damaged them.

Shelby enjoyed having future victims pre-loaded into the chamber. She would never pass on an opportunity as golden as AIDS poisoning. Though she was still high on Mr. Pinsent's murder, the afterglow of her killings seemed to shrink with each one.

A dialysis patient experienced an acute kidney injury following Shelby's tainting of the machine with bleach, but while the patient suffered incredible pain and expelled black urine, she'd miraculously survived the incident and was now receiving multiple hemodialysis treatments to recover her renal function. It was a grueling experience for the patient, which pleased Shelby, but the lack of a fatality perturbed her. She knew it would be best to lie low, but the urge to keep killing was only growing stronger.

Returning to the front desk, she checked in with the head nurse before clocking out. Having been asked to stay later, Shelby had worked twelve hours. Her supervisor praised her dedication to her patients as they said their goodnights.

Outside the hospital, a yellow moon hung low on the horizon. The darkness was coming earlier now that summer was gone. Shelby preferred it that way. It was always nice to cross another date off the calendar.

Once inside the sanctuary of her apartment, she changed into loungewear, poured a large glass of wine, and turned the TV to a true crime show. The genre was more popular than ever, so she was never short on specials about serial killers, mass murderers, serial rapists, thieves, and gangsters. These were not just her favorite form of entertainment, but her favorite types of people. She couldn't relate to folks without a criminal mind. They simply bored her.

The show she watched now was on Bonnie and Clyde. Not the most vicious of killers, but still a compelling story, particularly because of the romance between the duo, and the brutal nature of their deaths. Most people knew them as a bank-robbing couple, but they'd also robbed funeral homes, which titillated Shelby as she curled up on the couch.

"Bonnie and Clyde are suspected of killing nine police officers and four civilians," the narrator said, *"during the public enemy era of the early 1930s."*

Shelby stared at the black-and-white photo of the young couple on the screen. Clyde held Bonnie up in one arm as she smiled warmly at the camera. They looked like they'd just left the chapel after their wedding vows, but the truth was they'd been part of a deadly gang.

"Bonnie Parker was only twenty-three years old when she died from twenty-six bullet wounds during the famous police ambush. Clyde Barrow suffered seventeen entrance wounds."

Shelby shifted her legs, rubbing them together. The thought of violent death always stirred her, and she found the young couple's tragic demise rather enchanting. She'd never had a man who would die beside her like that. No one had ever proposed to her, and she'd never even had a relationship that lasted more than a few months. Though Shelby felt she was still cute, eligible bachelors did not pursue her the way they once had. Putting on extra weight probably had something to do with it, but she'd also become a homebody as her twenties ended. It wasn't like Mr. Right would just manifest in her living room. To make matters worse, she was getting older, and nothing disturbed her more than aging. It meant she was one year closer to being like her miserable patients; one year closer to that complete loss of humanity.

To cheer herself up, she opened the photos folder on her phone to browse through her favorites again. In one picture, she had her arm around the fresh corpse of Edna Gregory, whom Shelby had killed last month with an overdose of potassium chloride. She'd snapped a few selfies before alerting her supervisor to the woman's death. In another photo, she'd climbed into bed with Fred Strunk after killing him with a large dose of digoxin. The old man's eyes and mouth were wide open, his death mask one of shock and horror. Before snapping the selfie, Shelby had taken Strunk's dick out and held it like a joystick as she winked at the camera. The image always made her giggle. She browsed through some other shots of people she'd poisoned, some of which had survived the toxification. Others she'd brought to the brink of death just for the godlike thrill of resuscitating them—a form of resurrection.

The last photo in the album was of Shelby with Mr. Pinsent. Having left the old coot to die alone, she'd had to sneak into the morgue to take the selfie with him, but it'd been worth the risk to capture this keepsake. It was good to know he was dead, and even better to know *she* was the reason.

Shelby returned to the kitchen to refill her chardonnay. It came from a box but got her just as drunk as the expensive stuff. Opening the refrigerator, she almost expected to find human organs inside, like in the fridge at the hospital. A little more booze would help get her mind off work. She needed an improved balance of her job and her personal life, the latter of which she didn't seem to have anymore. Shelby didn't see friends or even hang out with people from work. It'd been almost a year since she'd been on a date, and even longer since she'd had sex. Loneliness had become a yoke about her neck and shoulders. It shackled her to herself, crippling her with a self-imposed deracination. How long had she been telling herself she didn't need a man to be happy? How long had she perpetuated this ridiculous lie? She wanted someone to do things with, even if it was just curling up in bed together to watch *Forensic Files*.

She finished another glass of wine while standing at the counter. The historian on TV continued, but Shelby wasn't listening anymore. She was lost in a cavern of thought, sinking deeper in search of an elusive solution.

This Bonnie wanted a Clyde of her own.

❀

The woman was one of the most infuriating crones Shelby had ever encountered, and that was saying something. As a nurse, Shelby was around ill-tempered geriatrics all the time, but Beatrice Vives was a special breed of witch, as repulsive in personality as she was in physical appearance.

"If my heart doesn't kill me," Mrs. Vives said, "this hospital food will. It's disgusting and inedible. Get it out of here—*now*."

Shelby bit the inside of her cheek to keep from snapping at her patient. She removed the lunch tray. Despite Mrs. Vives' complaints, she'd eaten almost everything.

The old woman sat up. "Fluff my pillows and turn them over to the cool side."

Getting behind her, Shelby looked upon Mrs. Vives' back, which was partially exposed through the hospital gown. Rolls of pimpled lard greeted her—a true horror. As Mrs. Vives continued her list of grievances, Shelby imagined smothering her with the pillow instead of prepping it to the bitch's liking. Vives was large but weak. It would be easy.

There was a knock behind her—three taps. Shelby turned to see a man standing in the doorway. He was well-dressed in a navy-blue suit and tie, with a pale blue pocket square poking out of the blazer. Though older, he was a handsome man, with salt-and-pepper hair and a lean build. She recognized him from yesterday, when he'd been shaking Mrs. Vives and swearing under his breath, a scene that had amused Shelby. She hoped he would be even more aggressive with the old fart now that she was awake.

"Well, well," Mrs. Vives said in a snide tone. "Look who's *finally* decided to visit his poor, sick mother."

The man remained in the doorway, holding his cane with both hands. Shelby imagined him using it to bash in his mother's skull until the crone's eyes bulged from their sockets and her teeth burst from her mouth.

"I was here yesterday, Mom," he said in a flat tone. "But you were asleep."

"Bullshit," Mrs. Vives said.

Shelby intervened. "It's true. I saw him here."

She didn't care about defending him, but she jumped at the chance to contradict the old woman, to take anyone else's side against her.

"Mind your own business," Mrs. Vives snapped at Shelby before redirecting her venom at her son. "Couldn't even bring me flowers or chocolates, could you, Bryan?"

"You're not supposed to have sweets," Bryan said.

"He's right," Shelby added.

Mrs. Vives scowled. "I said *butt out*! This is none of your business, young lady. Now get on your way before I report you."

Shelby turned her back on the woman and rolled her eyes for Bryan's benefit. He gave her a small smile, winking conspiratorially. Though he was older, having a good-looking man wink at her sent a shiver up Shelby's spine, and she warmed as she moved past him. His cologne tickled her nostrils. It was an old man's fragrance, smelling more like her grandfather's sweater than the spray can stuff guys her age used on their way to the club. Normally Shelby didn't care for cologne, but Bryan's musk was woody and masculine, the bergamot perfectly matching his classy appearance. She tingled again, surprising herself.

Was she so desperate that she was enticed by a man some twenty years her senior?

Given her disdain for old age, her interest confused her, but there was something about Bryan that set him apart from others in his age range. He seemed to have been transported from the previous century, like an actor in an old movie stepping off-screen. The draw was almost magnetic. She didn't feel sexually aroused exactly, though the man's boyish good looks and strong jawline made him easy on the eyes. He simply intrigued Shelby.

You're just lonely, she told herself as she left the room. *He wouldn't be so friendly if he knew you were going to poison his mom.*

CHAPTER FOUR

BRYAN PERUSED THE GIFT SHOP even though he wasn't going to buy his mother anything. The browsing was more of a case study. Seeing what was considered impulse buys these days, he was given a glimpse of normal human life, something inherently alien to him. Magazines he'd never read. ChapStick and bubblegum and other items he'd never used. Useless possessions like snow globes and keychains. They were all the adult equivalent of pacifiers—physical objects that provided a temporary salve to the unhealable wound of being alive. Bryan was not averse to such pacifiers; the gift shop simply didn't carry any that appealed to him. The only temptations were the bags of candy his mother wasn't supposed to have.

Bryan wanted to stuff her fat face full of them.

It would have to wait until she was back home. He couldn't let the nurses see him enabling his mother's poor health. But he didn't want Mom to come home at all. He wanted her to get sicker *now*, so she might never leave the hospital. Let her waste her remaining days in this sterile hell rather than rot away in the manor with her son waiting on her like a butler.

Bryan was a slave by blood. The old woman had pumped him out into this world, and for that he was supposed to owe her gratitude. But why? Existence was not something he'd asked for, and the trial run of it had left him deeply unimpressed. Being related to someone didn't mean you had to like them, let alone *love* them, and yet he'd continued this matriarchal charade, caring for the old woman without understanding his reason for doing so.

Bryan left the gift shop with a bottle of water. As he walked through the lobby, he waited as hospital staff escorted patients in wheelchairs through the front door. One nurse was the dark brunette who'd been tending to his mother earlier, the one who'd backed him up when Mom scolded him. Her cheeks were rosy from being outside in the cold, and as she wheeled her patient toward the dialysis center, he noticed how dainty the nurse's feet were in her tiny white shoes.

Then he noticed the look on her face. It was an expression she seemed to wear when she thought no one was looking, a bland deadness that reflected some secret, inner disdain. It was only a fleeting glimpse, but Bryan recognized a misanthropic haze about the girl. He'd seen that same look of swallowed fury in the mirror.

She hates this place, he realized. *She hates these people. Hates her patients.*

When someone opened a door for them, the nurse flashed an ironed-on smile—clearly she was more skilled at social cues than Bryan. His reclusive lifestyle had him out of practice. The nurse didn't have that same luxury of isolation. She still had to toil in the mire of other human beings.

Poor creature.

Bryan sat on the bench that circled the indoor fountain. He stared at the door to the dialysis center, hoping to see the dark nurse again, to spy her true form before she put her human mask back on. Children played on the other side of the fountain, oblivious to the tragedy of whatever had brought them here. Bryan ignored them. A few people tossed coins into the fountain, wishing for better outcomes for their loved ones. Bryan ignored them too, just as surely as the fountain ignored their prayers. He didn't check his watch or phone. He passed the time sipping water.

The bottle was nearly empty when the nurse appeared again.

She pushed a cart of medical supplies out of the center and headed to the elevators, not noticing Bryan, not noticing anyone or anything. The blankness of her expression was absolute—the pale cowl of those who were dead inside. She carried it well but couldn't hide it from someone like Bryan. He was too familiar with that low-level suffering to not recognize it, even when evidence of it was this minute. It was more than just the dull eyes of those who work in any service industry—in this case, the customers being the patients. The high demand of the job was likely a contributor to the nurse's unhappiness, but Bryan sensed her sorrow ran deeper than that. Her eyes never left the floor. She entered the elevator, and the doors closed over her with an eerie permanence, as if she were being taken away from Bryan forever.

You're projecting, he told himself. *You're seeing what you want to see in her, not necessarily what is there.*

Bryan tossed the bottle in the trash on his way out.

She's not even your type.

But he wasn't thinking about her like *that.* He'd watched and waited for her, but not in the way he had with the others. And all of that was a long time ago, anyway.

But it's always on your mind.

Or at least it had been lately. Perhaps it was his annoyance with his mother that had resurfaced his darkest memories. Could he be longing for a time when he'd felt more in control of his life, even if he'd not had as much control of himself? Maybe he was experiencing loneliness, despite never having accepted it as a concept.

You can't really think someone else could feel the way you do, right? Don't delude yourself. Don't embarrass yourself. You're far too strange to be relatable. You've learned that same lesson over and over—often at great personal expense.

But the thought had already embedded itself like a tick. Maybe he'd misread the nurse—he often misread people—but what was unquestionably real was Bryan's desire for her to be as he perceived her.

You want her to know the unexplainable, to understand the unbelievable.

Bryan grumbled as he approached the Mercedes—one of his late grandfather's many automobiles. The luxury car brought Bryan no joy. Few things did. Climbing in, he gripped the steering wheel and stared at the hospital, picturing the nurse wandering the halls in the same black mental fog Bryan faced in his home.

He wondered how many explosives it would take to destroy the hospital.

Dynamite, nitroglycerin, and lead azide powder. Ammonium nitrate fertilizer and fuel oil.

Bryan imagined the building cleaved in half, one side of it blackened and hollowed, the rest smoldering on the ground like volcanic ash. How wonderful it would be to have a bombing in this country that wasn't motivated by politics or religion. What would it feel like to have an unexpected force suddenly launch your body, to have everyone and everything around you burst in a simultaneous orgasm of fire? What could be more beautiful than an eruption of blinding light? It would be like witnessing the birth of a small, fabricated sun.

Though he'd never used explosives, Bryan could imagine fathering such a sun. If he put his mind to it, he could pack a van full of incendiary bric-à-brac. The question was whether to park it at the hospital and watch from a nearby rooftop, or detonate the bomb with him still inside the van. He envisioned charred children being catapulted from sickbeds, floors giving way to pitfalls of flame, towers swaying in cyclones of black smoke, bodies writhing beneath burning rubble.

There was nothing about the scenario he didn't like.

But it was just a scenario. One of many.

Bryan started the car and headed home.

"I want out of here!" his mother said. "You understand me, Bryan? I want to go home—*now*."

Bryan stirred in his seat. "Mom, you're not well enough yet. You need care beyond what I can give you."

"*Care?*" she huffed. "You call this *care?* These people feed me trash and pump me full of toxins. All this medicine, causing me twice as many problems as they cure."

"It's a process of finding what works, Mom."

But she wasn't listening. "They ignore my complaints," she said. "Try to tell me I'm crazy. They even make fun of my pain. They laugh at me, Bryan. They *laugh* at your *mother*."

"Come now," he said. "No one is laughing at you."

But he liked to think they were. He hoped all his mother's grievances about the hospital were valid. It would mean she was being deliberately tortured—like she deserved. But Bryan knew her too well to believe the things she said.

"I'm telling you," his mother said. "They make fun of me behind my back. They mock me and abuse me. And that Shelby—she's the worst of all."

Bryan raised an eyebrow. "Shelby?"

"The nurse you met yesterday. The one with the attitude. Little bitch gives me food I hate on purpose. And then she gives me the wrong medication!"

Bryan raised one hand to hush her. "Keep your voice down, Mom. This is a hospital."

"Some hospital! I'm telling you, the nurses screw up my medication. What kind of hospital is that, huh?"

"You're just being—"

In a huff, his mother sifted through the Styrofoam cups by her side, then held one out to him. Inside were various pills.

"See that?" she asked. "That's *not* my medication. I don't know what it is, but it's not what I'm supposed to be on."

"You're being put on a whole new regimen, Mom. That's why you're here."

"No! Damn it, Bryan, you're not listening to me. That Shelby girl has been giving me these instead of what I'm supposed to have. I think she's a drug addict. She's keeping my real medications so she can get high off them. And I'm gonna bust her for it."

Bryan sighed and snatched the cup away from her.

"Hey!" she said. "Gimme those back."

"Why, if you're not going to take them?"

"They're *proof*! Evidence!"

"The only thing this proves is you're not taking getting well seriously."

His mother ran red. "Don't you tell me what to do!"

"If you're not going to take your medications—"

"They're *not* my medications!"

"—then we're going to have to find some other way to—"

A knock at the door halted the argument. "Hello?"

Shelby entered the room, looking cute in her blue scrubs with the stethoscope around her neck. Her chocolate eyes met Bryan's, then she turned her attention to his mother, giving him a moment to look the nurse up and down. He noted how the curve of her hips seemed to invite a man. *Childbearing hips.* It was easy to imagine Shelby being popular with the boys, and yet there was no ring on her finger, and there remained that air of hushed unhappiness only lonesome women possessed.

"Speak of the devil," Mom said.

The phrase struck Bryan like an omen.

The devil, he thought, stroking his chin. *Devil, devil, devil.*

"It's time for your medication, Mrs. Vives," Shelby said.

"What a surprise," Mom said. "Another batch of poison."

Bryan winced at his mother's rudeness. "Mom, just take the medication."

A hint of a smile appeared on Shelby's face. As the nurse prepared a needle, Bryan's mother continued to rant, her complaints becoming frantic.

"I'm telling you, this is *not* my medication! It makes me feel strange. Shortness of breath. Dizzy."

"It's alright, Mrs. Vives," Shelby told her. "You're just experiencing some confusion due to the new med—"

Mom swatted at Shelby as she drew closer with the syringe. Mortified, Bryan rushed in to assist the nurse, pinning his mother down with both hands. She cursed, reiterating her paranoid delusions at top volume.

"Just stick her," Bryan told Shelby.

He was close to the nurse now. He could smell the lingering fragrance of her body wash. It was fruity, girly, *young*. But she wasn't as fragile as her aroma suggested. Shelby moved on Bryan's mother like a defensive lineman, putting her free arm across Mom's chest to subdue her as she jabbed her with the needle. The old woman bucked and let loose with a string of hateful vulgarities, cursing them both. When Bryan finally released his mother, she tried to get out of the bed but only swayed and fell back onto the mattress.

"Damn it, Bryan," his mother said, gasping. "She's . . . she's gonna kill me."

The old woman drifted off, the medicine quickly doing its job. Bryan didn't know what Shelby had given his mother. It didn't matter. If it knocked the crone out, he approved.

"She's just delirious," Shelby said.

"No need to explain. She's always delirious."

"I appreciate your help."

"No, no. I'm the one who should be thanking you. My mother isn't an easy woman to deal with. You've shown great poise."

Shelby furrowed her brow, as if she didn't understand, but didn't ask for clarification. "Sometimes people don't know what's best for them."

"You said it."

They looked down at his mother as she snored.

"She'll be out for a while," Shelby said. "Might be better for you to just come back tomorrow. Besides, Dr. Savalas thinks she'll be ready to go home by Friday."

Bryan formed a tight grip on the handle of his cane. "Actually, I was wondering if you might have a minute to chat."

"Oh." Shelby raised her eyebrows. "Are you sure you wouldn't rather talk to the doctor?"

"Positive." Bryan had never understood people's need to tiptoe around things. He preferred the direct approach. It saved time. "I'd like to talk to you specifically."

CHAPTER FIVE

SHELBY COULDN'T BELIEVE SHE WAS doing this.

But how could she refuse? The money was simply too good.

She'd never been an in-home nurse before, and wasn't sure if she was really qualified, but the man hadn't asked for any credentials or references before offering her the job.

He'd also made it easy to say yes.

Seventy dollars an hour, paid in cash upon each visit. She could make her own schedule so as not to interfere with her work at the hospital, and Bryan would even pay her hourly rate during her commute time. At the hospital, Shelby averaged twenty-five dollars an hour; even overtime pay was less than what Bryan Vives offered. The proposal was extravagant, and when Shelby arrived at the house she realized why.

The man was exceedingly wealthy. The mansion had over fifteen rooms, including a spa, a game room, a home theater, and two swimming pools. Walking around in it felt like visiting a museum. From online research, Shelby learned the Vives family came from old money, but while there was plenty of information available regarding Chet Gibson and his fortune, she'd found next to nothing about his grandson, Bryan. He had no social media presence. No arrest record or marriage announcements or other public history. Shelby wasn't sure what the man did for a living but sensed there was more to him than trust fund millionaire and mama's boy. There was a blunt seriousness to him that showed he could be assertive despite his awkwardness. He dressed beautifully, spoke elegantly, and had a mellow temperament—the opposite of his sea hag of a mother.

"It's just become too much for me, I'm afraid," Bryan said as Shelby followed him through the manor's dining hall. "With this most recent attack, my mother could really use the aid of a professional such as yourself, and, frankly, so could I. Caring for her has become rather trying."

"Totally understandable," Shelby said. "I mean, nursing someone with all your mom's ailments is difficult, even for us professionals. You've done a lot for her. She's lucky to have such a caring son."

The corners of Bryan's mouth curled, and he looked away. It was an expression Shelby found hard to read.

"I'm well aware of how abrasive she can be," Bryan said, leaning on his cane. "I do hope you won't take her comments personally. Unfortunately, she's like that with everyone."

Shelby didn't doubt Mrs. Vives was a bitch, but while the woman had been in the hospital, she'd shown considerably more loathing for Shelby than the other nurses. Mrs. Vives had even accused her of deliberately switching out her medications. While that was true, Shelby still resented the suspicion. It made her wonder why Bryan would choose her over some other nurse, but she was not going to risk losing the job by pointing this out.

As he gave her a quick tour of the manse, they passed by a room with an impressive organ. Of all the mansion's luxuries, this one struck Shelby as particularly interesting. It just wasn't the sort of thing you normally saw in someone's home, regardless of their net worth.

"You're a musician?" she asked.

Bryan shrugged. "I play a little."

She noticed sheet music propped up on the stand. "More than a little if you read music."

Bryan gave a small, humble smile, and they continued to the spiral staircase, then ascended to the floor where Mrs. Vives was kept like a caged animal. That's where the woman deserved to go—a human zoo, where people could throw peanuts at her. But Shelby had another idea of where to put Mrs. Vives. It involved six feet worth of dirt.

On top of the money, the chance to poison someone in their own home was a great incentive to accept this position. Though she would benefit financially from keeping the hag alive, Shelby could benefit even more substantially from spreading her bloodlust outside of the hospital. Eventually, too many patient deaths while she was on duty was bound to raise eyebrows at Merrimack Memorial. Shelby knew that, but she'd been unable to stop herself. A steady stream of victims was a prerequisite to her mental health. It would behoove her to mix up her *modus operandi*.

"You're welcome to all the amenities as well," Bryan told her. "Feel free to use the pools or home theater—just no guests, please. And help yourself to any snacks in the kitchen. I have a chef who comes by to prepare meals. If you'd prefer takeout, just ask, and I'll have whatever you like delivered."

Shelby blushed. "Mr. Vives, you're so generous."

"Call me Bryan. And please, think nothing of it. You're doing me an enormous favor."

"Alright, Bryan. Then you call me Shelby."

Stopping in the hallway, their eyes met, and he smiled down at her.

"Welcome to our home, Shelby," Bryan said. "I think you're going to be a wonderful addition."

He opened the bedroom door, and when Mrs. Vives saw Shelby, she screamed.

CHAPTER SIX

HIS MOTHER'S OBJECTIONS WERE JUST as colorful as Bryan had imagined. First, she'd cursed at them both, demanding Shelby leave the house and never return. Then, she'd insisted on speaking to her son alone. Having prepared what to say, Bryan countered his mother's arguments with practicality, being polite yet firm in his decision to hire the nurse. Though everything he told his mother was a lie, they were well-crafted lies, sounding more logical than Mom's insistence that a home nurse wasn't needed, especially one she didn't trust.

"You'll be the death of me," Mom hissed at him.

Bryan held back the urge to laugh.

He'd pocketed the pills his mother showed him while she was still in the hospital, and later researched them on his laptop. One capsule he couldn't identify at all, but he'd matched the others with images on healthcare websites, using their colors and engraved numbers to identify them. Mother was right. These were not the medications she was supposed to be taking, and from what he'd read, they had adverse side effects for people with heart conditions. Mom had been nasty to Shelby, so the nurse had given her a low dose of poison—not enough to kill the crone, but enough to make her sicker than she'd already been. The vindictiveness was amusing, but it was the pure sadism that excited Bryan.

Inflicting pain was the greatest source of serotonin. The blonde buried under the weeping willow tree could have attested to that, if she were still alive. Reflecting on her made Bryan sigh. By now all that fair flesh of hers would be long gone.

Time could be so cruel—far crueler than Bryan had been to anyone. It'd been decades since he'd behaved in such a monstrous fashion, but even at the height of his barbarism he never could have hurt his mother, despite how he often wished to—particularly in recent years as her medical conditions made her insufferable. This restraint perplexed him, given how he'd never felt close to the woman, not even as a child.

Beatrice Vives was sicklier than ever, but she'd never been *well*, at least not mentally. When she wasn't miserable, she was hysterical and vicious. The closest she'd ever come to happiness was her brief marriage to Bryan's father. Though Camilo Vives wasn't as unstable as his wife, he'd obviously been tortured too, as evidenced by his suicide by hanging when Bryan was only four. After that, Beatrice fully unraveled. This was why Chet Gibson had stored her and her son in the guest house all those years, taking care of his kin without having to spend any time with them, helping them without loving them.

Now Beatrice and Bryan had moved into the manor she'd inherited, and it had become Bryan's responsibility to care for his mother, a job he was incapable of and utterly despised. He secretly rooted for her death and regularly fantasized about ending her, but he'd never been capable of inflicting harm on Mom. Was it because she was his only remaining family, or was it because he worried committing murder of any kind would undo decades of discipline, causing all that hard-earned restraint to go to waste?

The Hooded Devil, Bryan thought.

It wasn't the name he would have chosen, but he supposed it could have been worse.

Devil, devil, devil.

The nurse had a devilish side. Though it would go undetected by most, Bryan had significant experience recognizing such things. The only question was just how deep Shelby's darkness ran. Was it a thin layer of brooding, or a river of menace that flowed into her core being?

He aimed to fish out an answer to that question, using his mother as bait.

Though Bryan had been incapable of directly inflicting harm on his mother, he had no qualms about someone else doing it. She always pretended to be in pain so she could better garner pity and dispense guilt, so why not give her a taste of the real thing? Mom deserved punishment, and Nurse Shelby might be just the tool Bryan needed to get the job done.

For too long he'd hindered his fantasies. A dive into his dark side was overdue.

He was also tired of waiting on Mom. The responsibilities of caring for her had become disturbing. A son should never have to bathe his mother or wipe her ass for her. The somewhat incestuous nature of such care could have traumatic repercussions. So even if Shelby didn't end up having the capacity for cruelty Bryan suspected, she would still prove useful—perhaps even invaluable. Her presence also allotted him more time to himself. While Shelby was upstairs tending to his mother, Bryan could lounge about the manor, stroll the property, and practice, practice, practice.

He struck the keys, raising a tremendous sound from the organ. The regal opening chords of Mendelssohn's *War March of the Priests* swelled within the manse, the organ working as a symphony unto itself. The march was dramatic in a manner Bryan appreciated, and it served as a perfect example of Mendelssohn's harmonic gift, making it an ideal test for Bryan's own skill. When played properly, the march lasted exactly six minutes. Bryan preferred pieces divisible by three. They made more sense to him. He'd first heard the piece in the opening credits of *The Abominable Dr. Phibes*, the cult classic film starring Vincent Price, one of many reels his grandfather had collected for his home theater. As a child, Bryan had been unaware of the movie's deliberate campiness and had taken the cliché horror storyline seriously. Now he credited it as an early influence in his becoming an organist—amongst other things.

It wasn't until the final notes that he saw Shelby reflected in the window. She was superimposed over the weeping willow, looking like a phantom within the golden leaves as they fluttered on the wind. Bryan sat up straight, staring at Shelby's pale reflection.

"You play beautifully," she said, breaking the silence.

Bryan turned to face her in the flesh. "You're too kind."

"No, I mean it. I've never heard someone play an organ like that before. I mean, like, not in person."

"I hope it doesn't disturb you."

"No. Not at all. Like I said—it's beautiful. You've really got talent."

Bryan didn't know what to say, so he said nothing. They looked at one another, but then their eyes fell away and the silence thickened.

"I've just given your mother her afternoon meds," Shelby said.

The way she said it made Bryan assume there would be more information, but the nurse didn't offer any. Standing with her arms crossed, she leaned against the wall and looked about the room, still taking in the manor's splendor. On her first shift as Mom's in-home nurse, Shelby had come dressed in her hospital uniform, but Bryan told her the getup was unnecessary, so she'd started wearing her own clothes. Today she was clad in all black. Blouse, jeans, belt, and shoes. Even her barrettes were black. Bryan preferred Shelby in her own clothing. Though not tight or revealing, today's outfit excited him. A woman's fashion was a window into her personality, and Shelby's penchant for black underlined what Bryan had ascertained.

"Has she been behaving herself for you?" he asked.

"Oh, she's no trouble at all."

The nurse said this with a plastered-on smile, the same costume worn by retail clerks. Shelby was just young and cute enough to pull it off. Her girlishness covered for the true self that lay beneath, a self that was nebulous and uninviting.

Bryan prodded. "Nonsense. My mother is nothing but trouble."

"It's okay." Shelby's smile fell slightly, a crack in the armor. "I've had difficult patients before."

"You're putting it kindly. Some people are difficult, yes, but others are downright horrible, aren't they?"

Her jaw shifted. "It's really okay."

"Only because decent people allow it to be." He stood, tucked in the bench, and tapped it with his knuckle three times so he wouldn't die. "My mother can be cruel. I've not brought you here to be abused, Shelby. If she's difficult to manage, I want you to know I'm not opposed to her being subdued chemically."

Shelby moved away from the wall she'd been leaning on and stepped toward Bryan like a dog sniffing out a new person. Looking him up and down, she seemed to be searching for something hidden, just as he'd tried to look into her soul.

"Are you saying you want me to drug your mother?" she asked, cocking an eyebrow.

Bryan thought he detected a hint of dark humor but couldn't be sure. If it was there, the woman knew better than to let it show in its entirety.

"I'm merely saying you can do what you have to," Bryan said. "I don't want you to hold anything back on my account."

"That's an odd way of putting it."

"Is it?"

She smirked. "I mean, you're sort of telling me to feel free to dope your mom up if she gives me any trouble."

"Not *sort of*. That's precisely what I'm telling you."

He stared at her, hoping to catch the darkness behind her eyes. Though she maintained her mask of normalcy, she didn't tell him what he was saying was unethical.

"You're just gonna let that hang there?" she said, still smirking.

"What do you mean?"

"You're just going to flat-out tell me to sedate your mom like it's no big thing? That if she's bothering me, I should just knock her out?"

He shrugged. "I just want what's best for everyone."

"But you didn't even ask me what I would use."

"Okay. What would you use, Shelby?"

"I don't know. Probably triazolam. Maybe diazepam."

"See, that's why I didn't ask. I'm not a medical professional, so they're all the same to me."

Shelby furrowed her brow. "You're not concerned about adverse reactions? I mean, wouldn't you want to consult her doctor before—"

Bryan raised a hand in a passive gesture to silence her. "That won't be necessary. You are my mother's nurse, Shelby. I will trust your judgment."

He deliberately kept saying her name. He'd learned that using a person's name made them feel more important. In Bryan's experience, it also made them more attentive, and when someone listened better, it was easier to form the sort of connection he wanted to have with his mother's nurse.

Shelby's smirk widened, her brow smoothing. It wasn't the empty smile she wore as part of her work uniform, but a coy grin that told Bryan more than words could. It reminded him of the conspiratorial glance they'd shared in his mother's hospital room—a coded signal, a secret between friends.

"Well," Shelby said, "in my professional opinion, sedating her would be best."

CHAPTER SEVEN

USING A WET RAG, SHELBY dabbed at the vomit dribbling from the corner of Beatrice Vives' mouth. At least the old woman got most of it in the pot Shelby had placed by the bedside in anticipation of Beatrice's reaction to the medication. One didn't have to be a professional nurse to predict the result of ipecac syrup.

The drug's only purpose is to induce vomiting, meant to be used strictly in emergency situations such as when someone has ingested poison. But Shelby was regularly giving Beatrice small doses of the syrup, mixing it into the diet soda she was always barking at Shelby to fetch another can of. Putting the syrup into a carbonated beverage gave it an extra kick because the combination could cause the stomach to swell. But even aside from that, ipecac was incredibly dangerous, especially to someone in Beatrice's condition.

Regular use could cause damage to the heart and muscles, and hers were nearly useless already. It also offered miserable side effects—achiness, stomach cramps, diarrhea, troubled breathing. Shelby even put it in Beatrice's drink when she was drowsy from the sedatives, which risked vomit getting into her lungs and causing pneumonia.

Beatrice belched. The stink rose around Shelby like swamp gas. The old woman moaned—not her usual *woe-is-me* sound, but a desperate, pain-addled groan that made Shelby tingle with glee.

"The treatments are working," Shelby said, grinning at the hidden meaning of her words.

Beatrice tried to object but could only gurgle and choke. Shelby raised the pot so her patient could spit, and when she was finished, Beatrice lay back on her mountain of throw pillows, eyes shut tight and breathing through her mouth. She reminded Shelby of some sort of diseased gorilla. Taking the pot of barf to the bathroom, Shelby snickered quietly as she dumped the contents into the toilet.

"Where's Bryan?" the old woman shouted from the bedroom. "Where the hell is my son?"

Shelby rinsed the pot in the sink. "I believe he's outside, getting some exercise."

"Exercise?" Beatrice coughed. "He doesn't *exercise*."

"Bryan likes to walk around the garden."

"Well, go get him out of the goddamn garden. I want to talk to him—*now*."

Shelby looked at herself in the mirror. "There'll be time for that later, Mrs. Vives. Right now you need to get some rest."

"How can I rest when I'm in such agony?"

"Don't worry," Shelby said to her own reflection. "I've got just the thing."

Beatrice huffed as Shelby returned to the bedside.

"No," the old woman said. "I'm not taking anything *you* give me!"

"Mrs. Vi—"

"Fuck you!" Beatrice said, giving Shelby the finger. White ooze pooled in the corners of her mouth. "I wouldn't let you nurse my cat!"

"You don't own a cat."

"You know what I mean. Don't get smart with me, you little bitch."

Shelby reached for her medical bag atop the dresser. With her back turned to Beatrice, her wide smile went unseen.

"I won't take any more of your pills," Beatrice said. "Not one!"

Shelby ran her finger along the syringe in the bag. She'd prepared it earlier, unsure when she would use the solution but preferring to have it at the ready.

"This isn't a pill," Shelby said, flicking the tip of the needle with her fingernail.

"Well, I'm not drinking any of your goddamn liquid meds either!"

So Beatrice wouldn't see it, Shelby cupped the syringe in her hand as she turned around.

"If you won't take your medicine," Shelby said, giving the old woman a patronizing smile, "I'll be forced to sneak it into your food."

"Then I won't eat."

"I find that hard to believe."

Beatrice reddened. "Are you calling me fat? How *dare* you! You know, you could stand to miss a few meals yourself there, girlie. You—"

Beatrice couldn't finish. Chest heaving, she began to retch. Shelby scooted the bucket closer to her patient, and Beatrice bent over it, dry-heaving, tears running down her swollen cheeks. Shelby jabbed the syringe into the woman's fat neck while her face was still in the bucket, and with a press of the plunger, the chlorpromazine concoction rushed into Beatrice's system. The old woman flailed with more strength than Shelby would have expected, knocking her into the dresser. She caught herself on the back of a chair as Beatrice swatted at the syringe sticking out of her neck like an acupuncture needle.

"You *bitch*!" the old woman roared. "You lousy little—"

"It's just something to calm you down," Shelby said, using her best nurse's voice.

"Bryan!" Beatrice turned to the open window. "Bryan! Help me!"

As her patient wailed, Shelby studied Beatrice, waiting for the medication to kick in. Chlorpromazine wasn't normally the sort of drug the user saw immediate results from, but at this high of a dosage and mixed with other antipsychotics, she hoped it would yield interesting results. Much of what Shelby did was experimental—little biology tests run on unsuspecting subjects. Chlorpromazine was used to treat schizophrenics and those in a manic phase of bipolar disorder, a phenothiazine antipsychotic that caused changes to the brain. It could also control vomiting, but a dose this large was bound to have the opposite result, for the other side effects included nausea, dizziness, shakiness, jaundice, and even regurgitation. But the side effect that interested Shelby most was uncontrollable muscle movements—chewing, lip smacking, blinking. Given that the drug wasn't prescribed to Beatrice Vives, the side effects would be the *only* effects. Shelby just thought it would be fun to add mental health meds to the mix, scrambling Beatrice's mind as well as her body. And to give the chlorpromazine an extra kick, she'd mixed it with Lexapro, a drug known to have major interactions with it.

Beatrice continued to scream for her son, but Shelby doubted Bryan would come.

The garden of Gibson Manor—now Vives Manor—was comprised of lush, open acres with small pathways beset with flower bushes. In the spring they would be beautiful. In October, they were the color of rust. But the red maples, dogwoods, and Washington hawthorns made for eye-popping foliage, their leaves casting blood spatters against the tombstone of the sky.

Shelby found Bryan sitting beneath the weeping willow. Orange leaves surrounded him like a rug of fire. He was scribbling in a journal bound in leather and didn't notice her until she was just a few feet away.

"Good afternoon, Shelby."

She nodded. "Bryan."

"Everything alright?" he asked, still scribbling.

Shelby glanced toward the mansion. Beatrice's open window was not far away.

"I suppose you must have heard her," Shelby said.

"My mother is not a low talker."

"But you didn't come running?"

Bryan looked at her, his eyes the color of glaciers. "I figured you had it under control. I trust in you."

"I appreciate that," she said. Still, she had to prod, had to know. "But most people would have come up to check."

Bryan held her gaze, then stared into the distance. He clasped his journal closed, and as he started to rise, he leaned on his cane, so Shelby assisted him.

"Don't get old," he told her.

Shelby smiled. "What does that even mean?"

"You'll find out."

She smiled wider as they started down the pathway, the loose pebbles crackling beneath their feet.

"You're not *that* old," she said.

"Old enough."

"Well, you look good for your age."

She immediately regretted saying it. Adding "for your age" could be taken as a backhanded compliment, and what was she even doing telling her employer he looked good? Was she flirting with him without even realizing it? Bryan had somewhat of a silver fox look, like Rob Lowe or George Clooney, but he wasn't exactly Shelby's type. She'd always preferred cocky alpha males with tattoo sleeves—wild men who seemed a little dangerous. She'd straddled the line between hating abusive men and loving a dominating male who would sexually bully her into orgasm. Bryan didn't check those boxes. He was courteous and even charming. Yet there was something dark about him, an inner blackness that kept Shelby engrossed.

Often the darkest men were the ones who didn't let it show on the outside.

"Thank you," Bryan said, flashing his handsome smile. "It's always nice to receive a compliment from a beautiful young woman."

Shelby looked away, hoping not to blush. Was *he* flirting now? A shiver rolled through her. She enjoyed these pleasantries and yet feared them, just as she feared any form of human connection, even while desperately craving it.

"So," she said, "why didn't you check on your mother when you heard her calling?"

Screaming was more like it, but Shelby didn't want to use that word.

"I suppose it's like the boy who cried wolf," Bryan said. "Mom yells so much that, eventually, I just learned to tune her out. And like I said, I trust you to take care of her now, however you see fit."

Shelby struggled with what to say next. She didn't want to ruin a good thing, but also needed reassurance she wasn't stepping into some sort of trap. She doubted the latter, but she still needed to better understand Bryan Vives.

"It's just . . ." she began. "Well, that offers me a lot of freedom. Much more than I'm used to."

"This is an unconventional situation. But in times of crisis one must find a solution, and all the better if it is a bipartite one."

"I'm not sure what you mean."

A gentle breeze caused Shelby to hug herself. Noticing this, Bryan removed his blazer and put it over her shoulders, ignoring her polite objections. It warmed her in more ways than one. No one had ever given her their coat before. She'd never been with a man who opened doors for her or made sure he was the one walking by the curb. She imagined Bryan was always chivalrous, whether or not he was romantically interested in a woman. He seemed like the sort of man who would consider it a prerequisite duty.

"I'm saying," Bryan said, "my mother and I are in a crisis and have been for some time. In my experience, that is what life is—a series of crises. When you're lucky, they come one after another, but more often than not they come simultaneously. You throw your back out, wreck your car, lose money in the stock market"—he snapped his fingers three times—"boom, boom, boom. Could all be in the same week or even the same day. All you can do is try to roll with them, and perhaps have a laugh at your own expense. Regarding my mother's health, I've tried to lessen the severity of the crisis. Initially I told myself it was for her benefit, but if I'm being honest, I've done it just as much for myself . . . more, even."

As they continued down the path, a drumroll of distant thunder vibrated the earth.

Bryan went on. "I am in the unusual situation of having more than enough money to afford solutions to this and most any other crisis, but for most people, unfortunate events are worsened by the financial woes they create. Hospital bills, increased insurance premiums, gambling losses"—he snapped thrice again—"boom, boom, boom. For every step forward, you get knocked back three. That's what life is—a series of bad things happening."

Shelby considered this. "That's not a positive outlook."

"I don't mean to be bleak, only realistic. I suppose one could conclude that life is, in itself, bad. But that's not the message I'm trying to convey, nor the mindset to which I subscribe."

But it was a mindset Shelby had found herself caught in. She'd been mired in despair a long time. As they entered the tunnel of desiccated bushes, Shelby walked a little closer to Bryan without realizing she was doing so.

"Bad things happen to good people," she said, "and good things happen to bad people. There's no justice. No karma. No God . . . at least, not one that intervenes."

"So then, what are we to do?"

New shadows moved across the garden.

"We intervene on behalf of ourselves," Shelby said, "and on behalf of others."

"To make the world a better place?"

"No," she said, flat and cold. "To make things fairer. To make things even."

CHAPTER EIGHT

"I WANT THAT BITCH OUT of my house," Mom said.

Bryan was alone with his mother in her bedroom, Shelby having left to do her night shift at the hospital. He understood why Mom was irate. She looked more than sickly now. She appeared putrid, a woman whose humanity had been stripped from her by drugs and illness. Bryan had always struggled to feel empathy, but he could at least understand his mother's suffering. But even if he had been capable of such an emotion, he wouldn't have felt any for the woman who'd birthed him. If anything, her anguish was mildly amusing.

"This bitch you hired is killing me, Bryan," Mom said. "Little by little, she's killing me."

Bryan took a deep breath. Though he'd just applied cologne, it did little to mask the foul odor of his mother's body. "You're being a bit dramatic. She's a nurse, Mom, not a monster."

"She's a cunt is what she is, and I want her gone."

"You know I can't care for you on my own."

"Horseshit. What you really mean is you *won't* do it."

"Mom—"

"Don't *Mom* me, you lazy, ungrateful bastard. I want Fuckface Nightingale out of my house. Understand?"

"It's Grandpa's house."

His mother reddened. "Don't gimme that shit! *I* inherited this house. You're lucky I let you live here."

"You couldn't survive on your own."

"Oh, yeah? Well, maybe I'll just hire my own team of nurses and butlers. People who know how to care for a sick woman."

Bryan sat in the chair beside her bed so his face would be level with hers. "You're forgetting that you legally put yourself in my care. I have power of attorney."

"Well, unless you get rid of Shelby, I'm taking you off that, 'cause if you keep letting her do this shit, you're clearly not fit to take care of me."

With those words, a tremor went through Bryan's blood, chilling it. He gripped his kneecaps as if they were a ledge he was dangling from.

"Perhaps I learned it from watching you, Mommy dearest," he said with a sneer. "How fit to take care of me would you say *you* were? How good of care did you provide me as a child?"

His mother paled. "I gave you a roof and three square meals a—"

"No, Grandpa did. He may not have loved me, but he did provide. You, on the other hand, couldn't be bothered."

"That's not fair! I was sick."

"No, you were crazy."

Her eyes went wide. "Bryan!"

"That's why Grandpa didn't want you here in his mansion. He tucked us into the guest house like a dirty little secret, hiding us to keep the Gibson name in good standing. He couldn't let his irrational, volatile, promiscuous daughter ruin the family's reputation."

His mother swung, trying to slap him across the face, but she was too slow and weak, and Bryan moved out of reach easily.

"How dare you speak to me this way!" she said. "You don't know what it was like for me back then!"

"Oh? Then who would know better? I was there for it all. All the imaginary bugs, all the manic spells, all the late-night boyfriends you brought home from bars."

"You don't—"

"You know, when Dad killed himself, he abandoned me. He left me with an emotionally abusive mother who drank too much and parented too little."

Mom kicked her legs like a child in a tantrum. "You shit! You don't know what it's like to be me! You don't know what it's like to raise a child alone when you're sick and your husband is dead!"

Bryan leaned in close. "Why do you think he did it?"

His mother punched the mattress but wouldn't answer.

"Why do you think Dad hung himself?" Bryan asked.

"Fuck you, Bryan."

"I believe I know. Would you like me to enlighten you?"

"*Fuck you!*" she screeched. "Your father was sick. Let *me* enlighten *you*. Suicide ran in your dad's family. His father shot himself. His little sister slit her wrists. His aunt jumped off a bridge into a fucking freezing river."

The weight of this new information struck Bryan like a baseball bat. He sat back in the chair and gazed out the window at the dying light of another day. They just kept getting shorter, the darkness strengthening, warning of the coming winter.

"So what were you gonna say, smart-ass?" Mom asked. "That Camilo hanged himself 'cause I was too unbearable to live with? Huh? Is that the foul shit you were gonna try and feed your mother? Well, fuck you, sonny boy. Fuck you and your stupid opinions. All you do is mope around here all day and piddle with that fucking organ. No job. No wife. *No future.* What have you done with your life, huh? What mark are you leaving on this world?"

Bryan thought of the headlines he'd clipped for the scrapbook hidden in the wall safe. He'd left his mark but could never brag about it even if he wished to.

"Some son you are," Mom said. "Some sorry excuse for a man, too. It's a good thing your father killed himself. I'm glad Camilo's not alive to see what a failure his boy turned out to be. If he weren't already dead, he'd die of shame."

Bryan swallowed hard as he continued to stare at the weeping willow just outside the window. He knew he should be furious with his mother for her hurtful words, but he only felt numb. It was a force field he'd constructed during childhood, a defense mechanism against the woman's emotional abuse.

He started toward the door.

"Fire that nurse, Bryan," his mother growled. "Fire her or I'm calling my lawyer."

Bryan paused in the doorway but didn't turn around to face her. "How?"

He didn't have to see his mother to know the look of rage she was displaying. There was no phone in her room, and she was incapable of going downstairs on her own to make a call on the landline. Mom also didn't have a cellphone. She insisted they were radioactive and caused brain cancer and hemorrhages. She didn't even like that Bryan had one.

As she started screaming more threats, Bryan closed the door on the old woman and descended the winding staircase. Once he was sitting at his organ, he started playing "Light My Fire" by The Doors.

Mom had always hated that song.

In the security of the bathroom, Bryan gazed upon the scrapbook. The old headline shouted with bold print, looking fresh even on the yellowed paper.

THE HOODED DEVIL STRIKES AGAIN
YOUNG COUPLE FOUND SLAIN IN PARK

Usually the memories aroused him, but today his mother's harsh words distracted him too much to truly enjoy the nostalgia. This had been one of his favorite homicides. The young couple—whom he later learned were Jason Azaria, twenty, and Monica Clark, eighteen—had been making out in Jason's parked car by the softball field after dark. Bryan had been young then, and strong. The car doors had been unlocked, and after sneaking up on the couple, Bryan swung the driver's-side door open, grabbed Jason by the hair, and stabbed him in the throat three times before the lover boy could even register what was happening. As Jason flailed, Bryan kept stabbing, sending the enormous blade of the hunting knife into his victim's chest and abdomen. At first, all Monica did was scream, but then she jumped out the passenger side and ran off in only her skirt. Without her shoes, she couldn't run well, and Bryan caught up with her easily. He slashed at her bare shoulders before snatching her by the hair, then yanked her head back to expose her throat. He opened it with a deep slice from ear to ear. Blood gushed, covering her small breasts like body paint, and the girl's screams became gargles as she dropped to her knees, clutching at the wound as it bled through her fingers.

Jason had called out for his sweetheart then. Surprised the man was still alive, Bryan returned to him, and Jason kicked him in the shin before Bryan pinned him on his stomach and hacked with crazed abandon. The newspapers would later report that Jason Azaria was stabbed a total of sixty-three times, not including the grazes and other cuts.

Bryan didn't rob his victims or swipe any mementos. He didn't rape or molest them or defile their corpses. His only desire had been to kill. It was an insatiable bloodlust he'd developed after Alice Fuller. Since her murder, Bryan had begun stalking and slaying random victims. Taking inspiration from slasher movies that had been popular at the time, he'd fashioned a mask out of a red pillowcase, magic marker, and a devil-horned headband from an old Halloween costume. Wearing it with all black clothing had given him an indescribable thrill. He'd felt as if he were in a movie, and when one of his female victims survived his attack and described his appearance to police, the press dubbed him The Hooded Devil, certifying his stardom.

Now in his fifties with a gimp leg, depression, and other undiagnosed health problems, Bryan had long since hung up his hood. He'd effectively retired from serial killing before the end of the previous century. The decision to quit came out of concern for his own safety. One victim had struck him over the head with a baton before Bryan could overpower him. Another had pulled his hood off, and Bryan had been especially brutal with her to make sure she didn't live to describe him, using a wrench to hammer her face until the skull cracked like a watermelon. One man had caught Bryan by surprise, coming home as Bryan was choking the man's daughter with her own nylons. If not for his pistol, Bryan might not have been able to kill the father fast enough.

He'd also grown worried about getting caught. A few close calls had riddled him with anxiety about hunting new victims. Bryan was not so much afraid of a death sentence as he was of life in prison. He didn't believe he could handle spending his remaining years in a cage with savage inmates more animal than man.

Perhaps more than all of this, Bryan had felt it was time to put The Hooded Devil to rest before the demon could devour him whole. But the lust to take young lives remained. Even while he managed to suppress it, the desire to kill continued unabated. Even now, decades after his last murder, Bryan still had blood-soaked daydreams. His fantasies always steered back to memories of his time as one of America's most wanted killers. Violent news stories were his pornography, and while he appreciated today's mass murderers, Bryan missed the golden age of serial killers. He longed for men like Dahmer, Bundy, Kemper, and Ramirez—and he missed The Hooded Devil. That masked slayer had taken sixteen lives across New England in the mid '90s—even though law enforcement only connected nine of those murders and attributed them to him.

Bryan flipped through the scrapbook some more, reliving the glory of his youth with a bittersweet smile. Now that he was growing old, he wanted to snatch life from the young more than ever, but even if he dared to unearth the hood from its tacklebox in the crawlspace, he was too weak to do what he once had. He would fail to perform and would only end up more anxious and unhappy than when he'd begun—or worse. The only way he could successfully stalk and kill would be with a firearm, but he'd tried that for a short time in his heyday, having stolen one of his grandfather's old war pistols, and found it grossly unsatisfying. It was too easy and impersonal, and now—at least in America—shootings were just too trendy.

There could be no resurrecting The Hooded Devil. That part of Bryan's life was over. Growing old meant one had to accept they couldn't always be what they once were. It was a standard clause.

Falling into the tar of self-pity, Bryan closed the scrapbook in disgust and exited the bathroom. Turning off the overhead fan, he was once again able to hear his mother raving down the hall, screaming demands he ignored as he pondered where to go from here.

For once, the old hag was right. He was stagnant, directionless, pointless. Bryan Vives needed help.

As he returned the scrapbook to the wall safe, the doorbell rang, lifting his spirits. He hadn't realized the time.

"You better not let that bitch back in my house!" Mom shrieked from her bedroom.

For a man with a cane, Bryan descended the stairs quickly.

At least he had one thing to look forward to.

CHAPTER NINE

STEPPING OUT OF THE SHOWER, Shelby ran her fingers across the scar on her abdomen. Having received it at such a young age, she'd hoped it wouldn't show as she got older, but it was too large to fade. Even all these years later, she remained self-conscious about it, and after gaining all this weight she was even more insecure about her looks. As she reached for a towel, she avoided her reflection in the mirror, even though it had fogged.

The bathroom was immaculate—certainly more extravagant than any she'd been in before. The shower had a seat and multiple nozzles, and it was big enough for three people. There was a whirlpool tub and marble counters with gold trim. Even the toilet was a work of art that included a bidet and seat warmer.

She hadn't planned on showering in Vives Manor, but Beatrice had been particularly disgusting today. In a way, it was Shelby's own fault she'd been splattered with the old woman's feces. She was the one secretly pumping Beatrice full of laxatives. But Shelby considered a little poo on her arms a small toll for seeing that crone wallow in her own filth like the fat pig she was. Shelby had been prepared to bathe Beatrice too, but the old witch insisted on washing herself once Shelby had escorted her to the tub in her master bathroom. Shelby believed that if Beatrice had been physically able, she would have gotten violent with her. She wished the old woman *would* strike her. It would give Shelby an excuse to fight back, to really put her hands on the bitch and show her just how much worse things were going to get.

Before entering the shower, Shelby had put her phone on the end table just outside the bathroom door. Bryan noticed this from the adjacent room where he was writing music. It was his first toccata in years. Shelby had not noticed him tucked in the farthest corner of the room. He gaped at the phone for less than a second before springing from his seat and shuffling to the end table as quickly as he could.

The phone was still bright, still awake—still *open*.

This was a rare opportunity he might not see again. Catching her phone before it went into sleep mode meant an exclusive look into Shelby's personal life. It would be a vulgar display of privacy invasion, but Bryan's scruples were warped enough to allow it. His suspicions about Shelby were strong enough to warrant investigation. Seeing what she was doing to his mother, Bryan had to know just how far the nurse was willing to take things.

Just how devilish was she?

Was she only mildly sadistic, or was she . . . *like him*?

The latter seemed impossible. Bryan had never felt comfortable sharing his darkest desires with anyone, for he knew he was alone in them, his cravings those of a demented mind. He was not so deluded as to be unaware of his own madness. But while he'd never met someone who shared his bloodlust, obviously others existed.

Bryan doubted Shelby's text messages would offer much. He skimmed them but found they were mostly work related. It seemed she was short on friends and family with whom to correspond. It wasn't until he opened her photos that he found something interesting.

There were the usual banal selfies people her age took. There were pictures of the fall foliage, a few memes, and dozens of hospital photos. Snapshots of pill jars, medical charts, IV bags, and machines Bryan didn't recognize. But these images were insignificant. What drew his eye were the pictures of Shelby posing with patients.

They were all selfies, and all shared an acute morbidity. In each photo, the patients appeared drugged, unconscious, or even dead. Some were ghostly pale. One had vomit on their chin. Shelby, however, was brighter than Bryan had ever seen her. Her cheeks were rosy and dimpled by a wide smile, her eyes sparkling like glitter. Joy seemed to emanate from every inch of the girl. It was in her posture and poses, a happiness so radiant as to seem alien coming from someone he'd always seen as brooding.

He remembered how he'd caught Shelby in the hospital room with his mother, and how miserable the nurse had looked while wheeling patients through the lobby. That glimpse of a dark side—and a capacity for cruelty—had intrigued Bryan, and looking at these selfies now, his interest in Shelby intensified.

Could it be? he wondered. *Could the people in these photos really be dead?*

They were all old. Not one of them looked like they couldn't collect social security. Maybe they were just resting, but if so, why would Shelby take pictures with sleeping patients? There was something about these photos that seemed celebratory, as if each shot was a personal trophy.

Bryan's chest shuddered with excited breath. He zoomed in on the face of an elderly man splayed out in his bed like a beached fish. His face was a death mask, eyes rolled into his skull, his body in a position that seemed unnatural to rest in. Bryan had seen enough dead bodies to recognize one. Beside the corpse was Shelby, her arm out to snap the selfie, grinning like she'd just won the Powerball.

Bryan noted the medical sheet on the clipboard in Shelby's lap. He zoomed in more, squinting as he tried to make out the name.

"Fred Strunk," he read aloud.

He scrolled to the next photo. In it, Shelby was positioned provocatively, pushing her chest out and pouting her lips. She'd lifted Fred Strunk's hospital gown and was holding his limp penis in her hand like a wilted rose.

Bryan wet his lips.

He sifted through the other pictures, hoping for more ways to identify the patients. A blue-hued woman was the subject of several photos, and in one of them, the medical chart at the foot of her bed was in frame. Bryan squinted.

"Edna Gregory."

He repeated both names so not to forget them.

When he came to a photo of Shelby posing with a man's corpse in a morgue, Bryan's suspicions graduated to certainties. One photo was a closeup of the man's toe tag.

"James Pinsent," Bryan whispered.

She wanted to remember their names, he realized. *She wanted keepsakes.*

It was something he'd always been tempted to do with his own victims but had been too afraid. He'd felt it was too risky to take anything that could be traced back to a murder victim. But he'd always regretted not harvesting mementos. The best he could do was revisit the scenes of the crimes now that the cases were cold. That and paw through his scrapbook. Shelby, however, had a digital photo album to relive whatever it was she had done, as if she were chronicling a wedding instead of the deaths of patients. It was much purer than his clipped and yellowed headlines.

"James Pinsent, Edna Gregory, Fred Strunk."

Hearing the shower stop, Bryan exited the photo album, put Shelby's phone back on the end table, and walked on to the study.

There was research to do.

CHAPTER TEN

EXHAUSTED FROM THE LONG DAY, Shelby headed downstairs after putting Beatrice to sleep with a midazolam injection. The crone had cried for help, but Bryan had vanished somewhere within the labyrinthine mansion. Though growing weaker, Beatrice tried to fight, but Shelby had been taught how to overpower a dangerous patient. She then followed the sedative shot with an injection of water laced with strychnine. Last year, she'd been surprised to find it available for purchase in some states, to be used in landscaping for pest control purposes. The highly toxic chemical was the preferred method for killing gophers and other varmints. She'd had to drive to Missouri to buy it legally, but using it on multiple patients had made it worth the trip. There were other pesticides that had proven effective—anticoagulants and zinc phosphide being two of her favorites—but for

Beatrice Vives, Shelby broke out the queen of poisons. She'd given the crone just a tiny dose, wanting to make her ill without killing her. This was a test run, another delightful experiment on a human lab rat.

Shelby had finished her scheduled shift at the manor. Though she was looking forward to watching the Investigation Discovery network with a glass of wine, she decided to take advantage of her free meal ticket so she could stick around to see the early effects of the poison in Beatrice's system.

As she reached the bottom floor and rounded the corner to the den, she spotted Bryan sitting on the sofa, his legs crossed and his journal in his lap. On the coffee table was an open bottle of wine and two glasses, as if he was waiting for someone.

"Expecting a houseguest?" she asked.

He stopped scribbling and greeted her with a smile. "Actually, I thought you might have a drink with me."

"Oh . . ." She stepped closer, and he motioned to the easy chair across from him. "Okay."

As Shelby took a seat, Bryan poured the drinks.

"From the cellar," he said, showing her the bottle. "My grandfather was quite the connoisseur of spirits. I know next to nothing about wine, but this is a twenty-year-old Château Lafite Rothschild, straight from Bordeaux itself."

"Sounds fancy," she said, taking her glass.

"Oh, it is. I looked it up. A bottle like this can run close to a grand."

Shelby's eyes widened. "*Jesus.* I've never had wine even *close* to that expensive. Most of mine comes from a box. Wouldn't you rather save it for a dinner party or something? Like, a special occasion?"

Bryan smiled. "That's exactly what I saved it for, my dear."

"I . . . I don't understand."

"This is a special occasion. Very special."

As Bryan leaned forward, his grin gave Shelby goosebumps. Was he finally going to make a move on her the way she'd been expecting?

The problem was, she wasn't sure if she wanted Bryan to make an amorous move. Shelby was a lonely woman, and it had been too long since she'd felt a man's touch, but Bryan was a good deal older than her. He wasn't *old* yet, but his advancing age was apparent. Right now, Shelby's hatred for the elderly didn't apply to him, but in just ten or fifteen years that would probably change. Bryan was also entirely too gentlemanly to be seen as dangerous, and danger was what got Shelby excited.

But at the same time, she appreciated his gentlemanly behavior; she'd never had a man treat her with such kindness and respect. He was a time capsule from a place where manners were taken more seriously, and chivalry was still the way to a woman's heart. And while he was older, he was still quite handsome, and she couldn't deny she'd had a few fantasies. There was a debonair charm to the older man she couldn't find in men her age.

However, he was also her employer, and this was a job she didn't want to put at risk. Had their relationship been different, she liked to think she might have been the one to make the first move, but she was too familiar with her crippling shyness to believe she'd be capable of that. She didn't see Bryan as boyfriend material exactly, but she may have considered a "friends with benefits" situation if she weren't concerned it would complicate their business relationship—or, worse yet, compromise her plans for Beatrice.

Shelby would never make the first move with Bryan. But if he was about to make the first move on her, how would she respond to his advances? While she'd sometimes daydreamed about it, she had no plan should it occur in real life.

She sipped her wine for an excuse not to speak. Bryan joined her, and as he drank, his eyes never left hers, even when she looked away.

"How is it?" he asked.

She smacked her lips. "I don't know if I'm sophisticated enough to really appreciate its nuances, but it's very good."

"I suppose it is," he said, admiring the glass. "I can't tell the difference between the fancy stuff and the cheap swill. Like I said, I had to look it up." He stared at her until she returned his gaze. "I looked up a lot of things today."

"Oh, yeah?" Nervousness caused her to take another sip. "About what?"

Bryan's eyes glimmered in the soft light of the chandelier. "James Pinsent," he whispered.

Though his smile was without malice, a coldness crawled up Shelby's spine at the mention of her victim.

"Also, Edna Gregory," Bryan continued. "And Fred Strunk."

Shelby gripped her wineglass so hard she feared it might break. She could almost feel the color leave her cheeks. She sealed her lips, afraid of what she might reveal if she opened them.

"I read their obituaries online," Bryan said. "I also found social media pages for two of them where friends and relatives posted little memorials. You see, I had to make sure they were really dead."

Shelby eyed the hallway leading to the anteroom. The front door wasn't far. Bryan would be too slow to catch her. But if she fled now, she wouldn't know the extent of his discoveries. Curiosity would feed her anxiety and stunt any course of action. Offering no expression, she watched the man in stoic silence, for no matter what Bryan might say next, Shelby knew he'd caught her.

"Please, don't be frightened," Bryan said. "Yes, I did some snooping based solely on suspicions. I now know what you've done, but I am no threat to you—far from it. I'm not going to turn you in or blackmail you. There will be no extortion. I pride myself on being a gentleman and have no desire to get anything from you in exchange for my silence."

Shelby furrowed her brow. "Then what do you want?"

Bryan reached for the bottle, and Shelby allowed him to refill her glass, wanting to stay on his good side. She needed more information before she weighed her options. If he meant what he was saying, she might not have to kill him—something she hoped to avoid. It would be too messy to take out someone who wasn't a sick patient. There would be too many questions, too many ways to get caught. She'd been in his employ. Police would investigate her if Bryan suddenly vanished. Shelby didn't think she could handle that sort of pressure.

His glass refilled, Bryan sat back in his chair and sniffed the wine.

"I have something I want to show you," he said. He nodded toward the oak cabinet beside the grandfather clock. "Would you mind fetching it for me? My knee has been especially troublesome today with this cold front."

Shelby stood but held on to her glass. If she needed to defend herself, she could shatter it and use the shard like a knife. Keeping her eyes on Bryan, she slowly approached the cabinet. Opening it, she saw a dusty tacklebox on the top shelf and sensed it was what the man wanted. She turned back to him with the box in her hands.

"Go ahead, dear," Bryan said.

He bit his bottom lip, showing an uncharacteristic nervousness. Though hesitant to do so, Shelby popped the latches on the tacklebox, holding her breath. She suddenly felt like a detonation expert cutting wires on a bomb. Whatever was inside, it was clearly a big deal to Bryan Vives. Perhaps it was about to be a big deal to her as well.

"Go on," Bryan said. "Open it."

She spotted sweat on his brow despite the coolness of the room.

"Are you sure you want me to do this?" she asked.

The question seemed to take him by surprise. He stroked his chin, then nodded. "Go ahead, my Shelby."

This term of endearment was a new one. By simply adding the word "my" before her name, he'd evoked tenderness and intimacy, as if he'd deemed her his own private treasure without the insult of claiming ownership of her. Even in this clenched moment, when stress was pecking at her every nerve, the expression warmed Shelby. To her surprise, her fear began to ebb.

She opened the box.

Inside was what appeared to be a small, red sheet. She glanced at Bryan, but he said nothing, so she lifted the object to unfurl it. The hood revealed itself to her, complete with the Halloween devil horns and crudely drawn demon face on the front.

Shelby had grown up with the local legend. The killings happened when she was just a little girl. As an adult, she'd watched documentary programs about the unsolved case and listened to countless podcasts that covered it. There were true crime paperbacks about it sitting on her bookshelf at home. It was a mystery as complex and chilling as The Zodiac Killer or Jack the Ripper, but it had happened right here in southern New England, and took place within her lifetime, making it feel more personal, more real.

Shelby put her glass down. Mask in hand, she looked to Bryan, and this time she held his stare.

"The Hooded Devil," she said in nearly a whisper.

Still sitting, he took a small bow. "At your service."

The room seemed to swell, and a shiver raked Shelby's flesh. Even as doubt surfaced, her heart insisted upon the reality her mind struggled to accept. Her thumb touched something crusty. Something had dried. The spot was a darker shade of red than the rest of the hood.

"Whoa," she said. "Hold up . . ."

Taking his cane, Bryan rose, causing Shelby to step back. She wasn't sure if she should fear him or not. If he was who he said he was, he'd done brutal things—many of them to women. Shelby couldn't imagine Bryan stabbing someone dozens of times, but if he was guilty, those crimes wouldn't have been committed by the man standing before her now, but by a younger, healthier version. Still, despite how his body may have changed, it was difficult to believe a man with his kindness could have ever been so barbaric, so monstrously and unwaveringly cruel.

Dark sides are hidden on purpose, she reminded herself. *John Wayne Gacy was a pillar of his community. Edmund Kemper was such a friend to the local police they didn't believe him when he tried to confess to the coed murders. And what about you, Shelby? Who would believe a mousy nurse could be a murderer? It's the quiet ones you've gotta watch—that's what people always say.*

"I'm sure you have many questions," Bryan said. "Just know you're in no danger. Not from me . . ." He pointed at the hood. ". . . and not from him."

"What do you mean?"

"Apologies. I wasn't implying that I have a split personality or anything like that. I was lucid when I did what I did all those years ago. Although, I suppose my sanity is up for debate, considering the gruesome nature of my crimes, but I can assure you I'm no Jekyll and Hyde. What I mean is, you're not in danger of me turning you in, nor are you in danger of me physically. I've long since retired from wearing that hood and what comes with it." He offered a humble smile. "Besides, I've grown too fond of you to wish you any harm."

Though Shelby remained cautious, Bryan's words had an oddly calming effect. She believed he meant what he was saying about not hurting her. Did that mean she also believed he was one of the most famous serial killers to never be caught?

"Why're you telling me all this?" she asked.

"The correlation is obvious, isn't it? We share something most people never would. We are both serial killers."

Shelby tensed again. "I'm not . . . I'm not a serial killer."

But wasn't she? Though she'd killed multiple people, she'd never thought of herself as a serial killer, but now she had trouble denying it, both to Bryan and herself. But what if this was a trap? What if he'd already notified the police and was recording all of this, trying to trick her into a confession?

"Shelby," Bryan said, "we all must learn to see ourselves for what we are. It took me a long time to admit to myself that I was what the press called me. That, like you, I was a—"

She cut him off defensively. "I don't know what you're talking about."

"Come now. There's no need for such pretenses. We both know the things you've done. And now I've shared what I have done—what I am. I've never told anyone what I'm telling you now. Can't we skip the tiresome denials?"

Again, Shelby was struck by the feeling Bryan was being honest. But she had to be sure.

She put the hood back in the tacklebox and placed it on the table. Stepping into Bryan slowly, as if preparing for a kiss, Shelby put her palms upon his chest. She felt nothing but his body, but she slid her fingers between the buttons anyway and tore the shirt open.

Bryan didn't even flinch. There were no wires taped to his chest, no hidden microphone.

"How'd you know about my patients?" she asked. "And about me?"

"It was just a feeling at first. A dog sniffing out one of its own. The more I observed you, the more certain I became." Bryan rolled his shoulders and exhaled, seeming to struggle against what he said next. "But then you left your phone open, and . . . well . . ."

Her eyes went wide. "You *spied* on me? You looked through my phone?"

Bryan nodded with shame, unable to look at her.

He's seen the pictures, Shelby realized with dread. Her jaw shifted. It angered her that he would invade her privacy, but she was even madder at herself for being so careless. She'd gotten comfortable around Bryan—perhaps too comfortable.

"I'm sorry," Bryan said. "If not for my suspicion you were a killer like me, I never would have pried. Please know it was only my desire to share my own secrets with you that led me to delve into yours. It will never happen again, and I do hope you can forgive me."

Shelby crossed her arms and tapped one foot. She was torn. Part of her wanted to run out of the house and never speak to Bryan again. Another part of her wanted to smack him for his intrusion. But there was another part—maybe the largest—that itched to confess everything to him, to finally have someone who could understand what she was.

If she'd had similar suspicions about Bryan, she would have invaded his privacy too. Being a killer was more isolating than anything she'd ever experienced or imagined. Now that the opportunity presented itself, she yearned to bond with another murderer, but remained nervous about revealing her most private secrets.

"How can I know you're telling me the truth?" she asked him.

"I worried you might not believe me," he said. "Can't say I blame you. Had someone approached me about my crimes, I'd be similarly guarded. I had hoped the hood would be proof enough, but I suppose anyone could make something like that. Luckily I thought of another way to prove I'm being earnest."

He looked out the window. Shelby followed his gaze. Decaying leaves blew across the browned yard, and the weeping willow seemed to lean as if trying to rescue them. Darkness was coming, but sunlight remained, though muted by ashen clouds.

"Join me outside, will you?" Bryan asked. "I've something that'll erase all doubt. It's my biggest secret. One I've never shared with anyone."

He surprised her by taking her hand, and she surprised herself by allowing it, even *liking* it. How long had it been since a man had held her hand?

Following him outside, Shelby was led to the weeping willow, where she noticed the disturbed earth shaded by the branches. A hole had been dug, about six feet long and a foot deep. Leaning against the trunk were two shovels.

"I'm sorry to have to ask," Bryan said, "but I could use your help with the rest of the digging."

A strange heat moved through Shelby's stomach and climbed all the way to her throat. Bryan handed her a shovel.

"Don't worry though," he assured her. "It's fairly shallow."

Shelby whispered, "What is?"

Bryan leaned on his shovel like a ghoul in an old horror movie, but his expression was one of marvel, of wonder, like a child searching his backyard for pirate treasure.

"Don't be silly," he said. "Why, it's a grave, of course."

CHAPTER ELEVEN

AFTER WASHING HIS HANDS FOR the third time, Bryan returned to the dining room. He'd been prepared to summon the chef to the manor for a celebratory feast—the kitchen was far enough from his mother's room for her not to be heard if she squealed for help—but Shelby had only asked for pepperoni pizza, so he'd had a large pie delivered. She'd gone quiet but didn't seem shocked by his confession, only processing it all. As they ate, Bryan gave her more details pertaining to the skeletal remains they'd unearthed.

"Alice Fuller," he said, sipping his wine. "She was my first love. Looking back on it now, I'm sure many of the boys at school similarly admired her, but at the time, I believed my love for her was stronger than anything anyone else could ever feel. You know how it is when you're that young. You think you're the first to experience everything."

He smirked. Shelby watched him as she ate, her wide eyes giving the illusion of innocence. She looked so much younger to him then, and he was once again reminded of his advancing age, the steady approach of the Reaper.

"Of course, I was far too shy to handle it correctly," Bryan went on. "I was a quiet boy. Not a total outcast, but still an odd duck. Poor social skills. Weird. Alice was this beautiful blonde. Freckles on her nose and lips like cherries. She wasn't the most popular girl in school, but she was certainly better liked than I was. Out of my league, one might say. I mean, what would she want with a boy from the marching band when she could have one from the football team, right? It's easy to see that now, but no bat is as blind as a teenage boy in love."

"So, what happened?" Shelby asked.

Bryan exhaled. "I tried to woo her."

"Woo?"

"Romance her. Prove my love."

Now it was Shelby who exhaled. "I'm guessing that didn't go over so well."

"The funny thing is . . . it *did* work. At least at first. What I lacked in coolness I made up for in charm. I discovered I could make her laugh and keep her interest when telling a story. And I was good-looking in my youth. Never short on female attention. Things were going well with Alice, so I invited her here. It was nearing the last day of school and the wild roses were lush and bloody in color. I thought she'd like to see them. My grandfather was away on business, you see, and Mom was with one of her boyfriends. So instead of going straight home after school, Alice met me at a nearby park, and we walked here to the garden."

Bryan paused, collecting himself as the memories resurfaced. Hearing himself speak of the incident after decades of silence made his chest constrict.

"Things were going swimmingly. Alice loved my grandfather's flowers, and I told her she could pick as many as she wanted. By the time we sat beneath the weeping willow, she had enough to fill a picnic basket. My grandfather would be furious, but I wasn't concerned. Only Alice mattered. She was happy, and when a girl is happy it brightens the lives of everyone around her." Bryan took another sip of wine. "She allowed me to hold her hand. I couldn't believe it, Shelby. The girl I'd been pining for was *holding my hand*. Honestly, that was enough for me. I was content. But Alice leaned into me, smiling and batting her eyelashes, and I got it in my head she was ready for a kiss.

"Only problem was, *I* wasn't ready. I'd not expected things to go so well—things so seldom did for me—and I wasn't prepared. But I didn't want to be the moron who *didn't* kiss the girl of his dreams when she wanted it. I didn't want to be seen as some shy virgin—particularly because I was one. I had to man up. And so, I kissed her. And she kissed me back." He smiled, reeling through the memory. "That first genuine kiss. Nothing else like it. There's no love song quite sweet enough to capture that feeling, is there?"

He looked to Shelby for confirmation, but she only offered a polite smile.

"Anyway," Bryan continued, "if I'd just left it at the kiss, perhaps things wouldn't have gone down as they did. But alas, I made a terrible mistake that changed my life and ended that of poor Alice Fuller."

Shelby leaned in. "Did you try to force yourself on her?"

Bryan's brow lowered. "Absolutely not."

"You didn't pressure her for sex?"

"I'm a gentleman. I would never force myself on anyone."

"Sorry—you don't strike me as *that guy*. But if that wasn't it, then what went wrong?"

Bryan folded his hands on the table, tapping his fingers in a series of threes. "I made an even bigger blunder than trying to cop a feel. I told her how I felt about her."

Shelby raised her eyebrows. "Oh."

"That's right. Being the young, love-drunk fool I was, I pledged my undying devotion to Alice, unloading months of pent-up passion. I told her I was in love with her. I just felt like this was it, that the kiss sealed our love. But, of course, I was taking it all way, way too seriously—much more so than little Alice Fuller took it."

"What did she do? Did she laugh at you?"

"No. As bad as that would have been, her reaction was worse. She got mad at me. I'd offended her."

"Offended her?" Shelby asked with surprise.

"Alice proceeded to tell me her father had taught her all about boys. He'd told me we'd say anything to try to get in her pants, and the boys who said they loved her were the biggest liars of all."

"Oh, no."

"Oh, yes. My sweet Alice turned on me. In her eyes, I'd instantly gone from prospective boyfriend to scummy pervert. And being the inexperienced idiot I was, I just kept trying to convince her my love was true. I kept saying sweet, romantic things, not realizing I was only making things worse. To this day, I . . . I . . ." He ran his hand over his mouth and chin, steadying himself. "I just didn't want her to run away, you see? I didn't want her to leave the garden—not on those terms. I thought if I could just get her to sit down and listen to me, she would understand, but . . ." He hung his head. "I never meant to hurt her. I loved her."

Shelby watched him intently. "But you couldn't let her go."

"No. I could not."

He refilled their glasses, and they each took heavy swallows.

"I took her wrist when she tried to leave," Bryan said. "She pulled free of me, and I grabbed her around the waist and held her close, still trying to convince her my love was true. That's when she got afraid, and when she screamed, something primal in me took over. By screaming, she was rejecting my love in the most hostile way, and I felt like I had no choice but to silence her, even though no one else was in earshot. Before I knew it, we were on the ground, and I was strangling her."

Shelby visibly shuddered.

"Is this all too horrible for you?" Bryan asked.

Shelby leaned in, lips parted, breath growing heavy. "No . . . no, please, go on."

"I'm only trying to make you understand. I felt no anger toward Alice, no hatred. I didn't feel scorned because I had not yet fully accepted that she'd rejected my love. I thought it was all a misunderstanding that would be smoothed out if she just sat down and listened instead of screamed. I only wanted to hush my sweet, little girl. I did not strangle Alice Fuller out of rage. It was passion—crazed and misdirected passion, but passion nonetheless."

Shelby pushed her plate aside, as if to eliminate any barrier between them. Night had fallen, and the golden glow of the chandelier cast brown shadows upon the nurse's face.

"And what about the others?" she asked. "Did you love them all, too?"

Bryan shifted his jaw and tapped his index finger on the table. *One, two, three. One, two, three. One, two, three.*

"No," he said. "Alice taught me the horror that love brings. After her, I never loved anyone again."

"But you continued to kill."

Bryan nodded grimly.

"Why?" Shelby asked.

"Because . . . because I had grown to hate love."

Silence fell between them, heavy as cast iron. They didn't nibble their food or sip their beverages. Bryan had stopped tapping his fingers. There was only this mute deadness to underline all that had come before it.

Finally, Shelby broke the spell. "Because love worked for others, but it hadn't worked for you. Love betrayed your trust in it, and yet it proved true for other people. You resented that. Is that it?"

He shook his head. "You make it sound like petty envy."

"If I'm wrong, say so."

"You're asking me to answer a question I've been asking myself for the last four decades."

"Are you saying you don't know the answer?"

"I'm saying I don't believe there is one. Not a *single* answer, anyway."

"But you said you were motivated to kill by a hatred of love."

He wagged his finger. "No, no. I had grown to hate love, but I wouldn't consider that my motive."

"Then why'd you say it?"

"Because . . ." He sighed with frustration. "Because . . . alright, Shelby. Some of what you're saying is correct. I did resent that others could express love correctly, whereas I had ruined it just by using the word. I was envious of happy young couples. I hated that they got to have what I couldn't with Alice. But it still wasn't anger that drove me. It was still *passion*." He took a long drink, hoping Shelby would interject, but she only waited for him to continue. "At that time in my life, strangling Alice in a fit of passion was as close to expressing love physically as I'd ever gotten. I think, therefore, it warped me. I was too afraid of falling in love with another girl, afraid I'd fail again the way I had with Alice. But I wasn't afraid to kill. Being rejected by Alice had hurt me. Killing her had not. If anything, it brought me pleasure, even though I'd not wished her any harm. Murdering Alice was so physically intimate it served as a substitute for sex."

"But The Hooded Devil wasn't a sexual sadist," Shelby said. "He wasn't a Ted Bundy type."

"I am not a rapist. As I said, I find sexual assault abhorrent."

"But you came to associate sex and violence."

"No. I came to associate love and destruction. There is a difference."

Shelby's dark eyes studied him. "I'm not sure I understand."

"That's quite alright." He shrugged, feeling the wine kicking in. "I don't fully understand it myself. All I can say is love hurt me, so I chose to hurt love in return. Other boys had loving families. I did not. Other men had loving wives. I felt I never could." He leaned in closer until he could see his shadow reflected in her eyes. "It was never the lovers I wanted to murder, Shelby. It was love itself."

CHAPTER TWELVE

BRYAN HAD CONVINCED SHELBY OF the truth. It was hard to deny it after they'd dug up the human remains in his yard. After revealing the evidence, Bryan had thrown dirt over the corpse again, and she'd helped him until they'd refilled the grave.

Incredibly, he'd never been caught for the murder. He explained that while he'd been questioned by police, so had many other students, including several of the girl's male suitors. No one else had known about Alice's plans to meet with Bryan that day. It'd happened spontaneously. With no criminal record, and given his grandfather's standing in the community, investigators hardly gave young Bryan Vives a second glance. The police seemed to believe Alice had run away, that she'd taken off with a boyfriend no one knew about.

"So, what happens now?" Shelby asked as they strolled down the hallway. "We know each other's dirty secret, but where do we go from here?"

"I never thought I'd meet someone who had the same urges I do," Bryan said. "It feels good to be able to talk to someone about it. Amazing, really. Why don't you try it? Tell me something you've never been able to tell another person. Maybe, if we can share our darkest truths, we can help each other."

Shelby shook her head. "I'm not looking for therapy. I'm not insane."

"That's not what I mean. I'm not saying we can help each other recover from what we've done. I'm saying . . . we can help each other do what we do best, what we were born to do."

Shelby swallowed hard.

"*Kill*," Bryan confirmed. "It's our fate, Shelby. Don't you see? We were given life so we might take it from others."

Shelby looked away, still uncomfortable with someone knowing her secret. But she couldn't deny it. Bryan was right—she *was* relieved to have someone to share this side of herself with. It was just going to take some getting used to.

"I've retired from it, you know," Bryan said. "Haven't killed anybody in over fifteen years. The Hooded Devil just . . . vanished. Some think he died or went to prison for other crimes. Not the case."

"What happened? Why'd you suddenly stop?"

"It wasn't so sudden. It was a decision I came to gradually. There were a variety of reasons to stop killing, just as there were a variety of motives that led me to kill in the first place. But the cons came to outweigh the pros—at least that's what I felt then. But even while I abstained, I never stopped thinking about it. Lately I've been living in my memories of murder. Maybe it has something to do with getting older. A midlife crisis of sorts."

"Maybe you're just trying to feel young again."

He stopped walking and faced her. "Exactly. And meeting you—a young killer—has only thrown fuel on that fire."

They shared another heavy pause. The hallway was cool and dimly lit. Portraits of Bryan's long-dead relatives hung on the walls like an art exhibit, all those dead eyes falling upon them.

Bryan smirked. "Do you know why I hired you, Shelby?"

"Um . . . you needed a nurse to take care of your m—"

"To *kill* my mother." His smirk became a charming smile. "I wanted someone to *kill* my mother. And that is what you're doing, isn't it? Slowly but surely, you're poisoning my mother to death."

All the blood left Shelby's cheeks. She'd dealt with the family members of her victims before, but they'd had no knowledge of her lethal actions.

She struggled for words. "Bryan . . . I . . ."

He waved her apology away. "It's quite alright, my dear. I want you to do it."

She could breathe again, but her mind was only further scrambled. She'd suspected Bryan cared little for his mother based on his apathy toward her suffering, but Shelby had not known he was wise to her intentions, let alone that he approved.

"Doing it myself would be more than I could handle," Bryan explained. "She's a wretch of a woman, but she's still my mother. You only get one, right?" He put his hands on Shelby's shoulders. "I didn't hire a nurse. I hired an angel of death."

Shelby wet her lips. "It's only assisted suicide if the patient wants to die. Your mother has made it clear she wants to live."

"I don't care what my mother wants."

"She's also made it clear she knows I'm torturing her and feels you're doing nothing to stop me."

Bryan shrugged. "Good."

"How is that *good*?"

"I'm glad she knows what's happening. Let there be no confusion. I want her to know she's being murdered."

Shelby looked up at him in wonder. The closer they stood, the taller he appeared, and his shadow fell upon her like a coming storm. His hands remained on her shoulders, cupping them in a perfect fit, as if they had molded these parts of their bodies for this very purpose, for this exact moment. It surprised her how strongly she hoped he wouldn't let go.

"Maybe you're right," she said. "Maybe I should share something with you. A secret."

He didn't speak, only waited. His hands stayed on her.

"I'm a mother too," she said.

She let that sink in. Bryan remained mute, but his eyes showed kindness and understanding, and that drew Shelby in deeper, opening her like a blooming flower plucked from his garden.

"I became a mom when I was seven years old," Shelby confessed.

Bryan's eyes widened. *"Seven?"*

"I know. It sounds impossible, but I went through what's known as precocious puberty. Rare, but not unheard of. It's a medical condition that affects about one in ten thousand children. Girls who have it physically develop much faster than normal. I started growing breasts at the age of five and had my first period just before my sixth birthday." She took a deep breath. "I've never told anyone who got me pregnant. I was not raped the way people suspected. My father never touched me. No one attacked me. I *chose* to have sex. Yeah, I was only seven, but I was flooded with hormones and had the desire. I know now that a child can't consent, and it was with an older boy, but even he was still a child himself, being just twelve. Just two dumb kids who threw caution to the wind and paid for it. Or, at least, I did."

"What happened then?" Bryan asked.

"I got pregnant. And eventually, my parents found out. Of course, they were mortified. I guess I should've been too, but I just wasn't. My father was particularly cold to me during that time. After a lot of talk, it was decided that it would be more traumatic—and potentially more dangerous—for me to have it aborted than for me to deliver it. But because of my small size, I had difficulty during the birth, and ended up needing a C-section."

She sighed, and Bryan tightened his grip on her shoulders in a way that made her feel secure. His touch spoke without words, saying *I'm here* and *I care*. She lifted her shirt and pushed down the waist of her pants to reveal the old scar.

"I never did learn the baby's gender," Shelby said. "They drugged me up for the pain and when I came around, my baby was gone. My parents decided without me to give the baby up for adoption, and 'cause I was just a kid, I had no say. It was *my baby*, and my parents just gave it away. I've never forgiven them for that."

His hands moved from her shoulders down her arms and gave them a gentle squeeze. Shelby moved closer to him without realizing it, and his aroma entombed her in a comforting fog.

"Is this where your anger stems from?" Bryan asked. "Is this what drives you to kill?"

"I've been asking myself why I kill for a long time and still don't really have an answer. Guess I'm like you, huh?" She started playing with his tie, staring at it. She felt suddenly bashful, small. "We've all got trauma, but not everyone is driven to kill by it, right? I mean, what happened with my folks and my baby definitely screwed me up, but I wouldn't go so far as to call it a motive."

"Some things can't be explained, my Shelby."

Their eyes locked.

"I kill the sick and the elderly," Shelby said. "I'm not totally sure why I do it, but I sure as hell enjoy it. Maybe it's 'cause they disgust me. I mean, shit, these are people who should be dead already. I just give them that little extra push their bodies need. But it's not mercy. I'm not putting them out of their misery. I either increase the misery they're already in, or I create all new miseries that make their old ones seem like a cakewalk by comparison."

"You want them to suffer," Bryan said, grinning.

"They *deserve* to suffer."

"Doesn't everybody?"

They broke into giggles. Bryan put his arms around her now, pulling her in for an embrace. She pressed her cheek against his chest and put her arms up around his neck as if they were about to slow dance. There was a vague sense of romance to this newfound intimacy, but more than anything else Shelby just felt safe, as if she'd finally found her way home after a long, lonely journey. It was not so much that it felt good to share, but that it felt good to be *understood*.

"You created life with your baby," Bryan whispered. "But they took it away from you. Now you take away the lives of others. Nature finds a balance."

"You think that's why I do it?"

"I can't tell you why. Only you can."

Shelby exhaled. "Maybe there is no explanation . . . but maybe we don't need one. Maybe it doesn't matter. What if nothing does?"

She gripped him tighter, and they held one another in the darkened hall, and this time, when silence returned, it was no longer uncomfortable.

They simply breathed. Simply *were*.

Then the screams of Beatrice Vives broke the spell.

CHAPTER THIRTEEN

"WILL YOU DO IT TONIGHT?" Bryan asked as he followed Shelby up the stairs. "Will you kill her?"

They reached the landing and Shelby stopped before the hall to his mother's room.

"What's the rush?" she asked.

Her playfulness made Bryan giddy. He couldn't help but chuckle, and he put his hand over his mouth out of fear his mother might hear him even above her wailing.

"She's your mother," Shelby said. "But she's my patient . . . my victim."

Bryan nodded. He respected that. He had to.

"Besides," Shelby went on, "I get the feeling you want the bitch to suffer."

Bryan stared into space, considering this.

"You're making her pay for something," Shelby said. "What?"

Bryan shrugged. "For everything, I suppose."

"But you can't punish her yourself."

"No, but I am punishing her by allowing you to. By ignoring her pain, I'm tacitly inflicting more of it."

"But you don't want it to be hands-on. You don't want to kill her yourself."

He shook his head. "I suppose I'm just too afraid."

"That it will haunt you?" Shelby asked, though it sounded more like a statement than a question.

"Yes."

"But at the same time, you've wanted to kill again. You've been fantasizing about getting back in the game."

He offered a sad sigh. "That's all they are—fantasies. I'm too old and weak for a comeback, what with needing a cane to walk and everything. I can't go stalking lovers' lanes like I once did."

"You don't have to. Maybe you can't physically overpower people the way you once did, but there's more than one way to skin a cat. Have you ever thought of using poison?"

"Not really."

She took his hand. "Allow me to demonstrate."

As Shelby led Bryan to his mother's bedroom, his mind reeled, flashing back to that sunny day long ago when another young girl had taken his hand. They'd frolicked through the garden, Alice pulling him into her—body and soul—until he was hers completely.

And this too will end in death, Bryan thought.

The notion came without bitterness. It only confirmed what he'd already come to believe about the inexorable collision of love and destruction. Life had repeatedly taught him this same lesson. *Everything* was subject to entropy. He'd come to expect things to never quite work out, and sadly, the universe never proved him wrong.

But Bryan still tried to enjoy whatever fleeting moments of happiness life offered. If he didn't, what was the point of living?

Entering the bedroom, Bryan saw his mother, and joy struck his heart. She was halfway out of the bed, her head against the hardwood floor, her big ass pointing toward the heavens like some repulsive weathervane. The room reeked of feces and the floor beside the bed was slick with vomit. Mom looked up at him with eyes so bloodshot they reminded Bryan of Christopher Lee as Dracula from his grandfather's movie collection. Weak and contorted on the edge of the bed, she was unable to move. Bryan delighted in wondering just how long she'd been stuck like this.

"Goodness, Mom," he said in mock sympathy. "That can't be comfortable."

She gurgled through mucus, cursing unintelligibly.

"Let's get you back in bed," Shelby said, putting on her caring nurse façade.

Mom groaned as they lifted her. The mattress was filthy, splattered with a variety of bodily fluids. The bedpan had overflowed. There was blood in it.

"Please," his mother murmured. "Please . . . help me."

Shelby patted her. "There, there."

Mom flinched at the nurse's touch. Instead of spewing her usual hatred, she cowered away from Shelby, a mouse cornered by a snake.

"Please," Mom said. "I . . . I can't take any more. Take me . . . take me to the hospital."

"It's going to be alright, Beatrice," Shelby said. "There's no need for you to go back to the hospital when you're receiving the same care at home. Now just relax and I'll prepare a shot for you to help—"

"No!" Mom turned to her son in desperation. "Please! She's killing me, Bryan. She's *killing* me!"

Bryan and Shelby exchanged a glance like two kids trying not to laugh in class. Shelby retrieved her nursing bag and withdrew a syringe.

"It's just the medicine, Mom," Bryan said. "It's confusing you. Don't worry. That'll pass."

"*What?*" his mother asked with wide eyes. "No, no, no! Look at me. Look at this room. She's poisoning me. If you don't stop this, I'm gonna *die*. Please, Bryan . . . my son . . . my only son . . . you gotta help me."

As Shelby prepared the shot, Bryan went to his mother's bedside. The old woman disgusted him. Shelby had been right. People like this should be dead already. Despite the foul stench, he bent over so their faces were close.

"You worry too much," he said. "First you think the house is infested with insects that are going to eat you, and now you think a professional nurse is out to get you. It's paranoid delusions. I know you're suffering, but it's your poor health that's causing it, not the treatments."

His mother tried to object, but Bryan put his finger to her lips and shushed her.

"Don't talk," he said. "Just listen."

Her face went slack with dread.

"These treatments are the only thing keeping you alive, Mom," he said, staring into her eyes. "You made me your caretaker. It's up to me to decide what's best for you and what treatments you deserve."

His mother went pale. Her lips trembled but made no words, only nervous mumbles to express her rising fear. In her gaze, Bryan saw the sweetest shock, the most delicious fright. It made him quiver. After a lifetime spent enduring this maniac, at last he had reconstructed the dynamics of their family. He held all the power now. The child had become the parent, and the parent the child.

He thought of the conversation he'd had with Shelby.

We intervene on behalf of ourselves, she'd said, *and on behalf of others. To make things fairer. To make things even.*

"Now hold still," he said, pinning his mother down.

Shelby flicked the syringe and gave it a little squirt. As Mom cried out, her nurse only smiled.

"You're going to feel a little pain now," Shelby said.

The needle dribbled as it approached the crook of Mom's arm, the tip glistening with a fresh dose of horrors. Her skin ran with goosebumps as she tried to twist away, but Bryan held her in place, and as the needle went in, Mom screamed and gnashed her teeth. She stared up at him with those red eyes, and Bryan stared back at her, his gaze unwavering and unapologetic, his face a cold, blank death mask.

But inside he was glowing because Shelby was right.

There really was pleasure to be found in poisons.

"What sort of killer do you consider yourself to be?" Bryan asked, adjusting his sunglasses.

They were out on the veranda on a day of unseasonable warmth, the sun shining, the fallen leaves steaming from the previous night's rain.

Shelby sipped her latte as she contemplated his question.

"What do you mean?" she asked.

"The motives of serial killers are often divided into four specific categories: mission-orientated, visionary, hedonistic, and power hungry. There's plenty of room for overlap, but these are the generally agreed upon archetypes."

"Hmm. I dunno. Which one were you?"

Bryan puffed his cigar. "I'd like to think I was a visionary, but more likely it was just hedonism. At least after Alice. Her death was mission-orientated."

Shelby considered this. "I must be a power-of-control killer. I like being the hand of fate. At the hospital, sometimes I kill my patients, other times I push them to the edge of death just to bring them back to life."

"Must make you feel like Dr. Frankenstein," he said with a smile.

"I guess. I always thought of myself as a Reaper."

"Is that why you only kill the elderly? Because you feel it's their time?"

She shook her head. "I don't think that's it. I just kill old people because I hate them."

"I can relate to that. I always targeted young people, particularly ones in love. Even though I was young too, I hated them. Now that I'm getting old, I envy their youth, so I hate them all the more. If ever I was to kill again, I'd want to go after these stupid kids in their twenties." He looked at her. "No offense to your generation."

"Doesn't bother me. Besides, I'll be thirty this week."

"Still young."

"It's all relative. But I sure don't *feel* young anymore."

Bryan chuckled. "Well, strap in, because it only gets worse. One thing I remember my father telling me on one of my birthdays was to enjoy life because it goes by fast. Best advice he ever gave me. Funny it came from a man who killed himself."

"I am sorry about that, Bryan."

"That's all in the past now," he said with a dismissive wave. "But it is interesting to reflect upon. When I was a kid, I didn't realize just how screwed up my homelife was. I was unhappy, but I thought a screaming mother and a father who took his own life were just how families were. I thought all families hated one another, just as my extended family hated my mother and me. It wasn't until I was in my thirties that I realized how dysfunctional my family really was."

Shelby wasn't sure what to say to that. The sadness surrounding Bryan Vives' life was a lingering fog that was noticeable even when he was in a good mood. She felt for him but had no good ideas on how to help him—other than ridding him of his toxic mother.

Bryan suddenly changed the subject. "You need to delete those pictures, Shelby."

She blinked with surprise. "What?"

"The photos on your phone. The ones of your victims. You must delete them. They're incriminating evidence."

She scoffed. "Are you kidding me? What about the *dead body* in your yard?"

"That's different. When I did that, I was just a boy. I didn't know any better then, and now it's riskier to move her than let her stay where she is. I kept no mementos from any of the killings that came after Alice. My only keepsakes are the newspaper clippings."

"Well, good for you, but I love my photos."

"Then use a Polaroid—something that doesn't keep a digital record."

She leaned toward him. "Bryan, I don't kill the way you did. I'm a nurse whose murders slip under the radar, not a knife-wielding man in a red hood. I don't need to be as careful."

"It's just that it's unnecessarily reckless."

"No, it's a necessary evil. Those pictures help me relive the moment. Without them as a substitute for the act, I'd be killing people every day."

"Alright," Bryan said, rocking his chair. "Forgive me if my mentoring isn't welcome. I only want to help you."

"I know," she said with a grin. "And I know I can learn from you. You killed nine people and never got caught, so you must've done something right."

"Actually, it was sixteen. They just never linked the other seven to me."

"My point is, you clearly know what you're doing. But you had your moment in the sun. This is my time, and I have to live my life my own way."

He nodded. "I respect that."

"And I respect you. There's still much you can teach me . . . and perhaps I can teach you things, too."

"Oh?"

"Sure. I mean, this is a different age we're living in. You've spent so much time as a hermit in this castle of yours. The world has changed. If you want to get back in the game, you'll need to be ready for it."

"Oh, my sweet Shelby," he said, shaking his head. "You flatter me by assuming I could ever return to my life as The Hooded Devil."

"But you *can*. That's what I want to show you, what I think I can teach you." Excited, she reached out and patted his leg. "We'll work together. I'll teach you my ways, and you can teach me yours."

Bryan flashed his handsome smile. He appeared older in the natural light of day, but not so old as to be worn out and forgotten.

"You may not be able to stab and choke young lovers anymore," Shelby said, "but you sure can poison people. The Hooded Devil could return with a whole new method of murder. And it can begin with your mother."

Bryan leaned forward and put his hand over hers. Finally, he nodded. "Alright. You do what you do best with Mom, and I'll be along for the ride. You can show me your way . . . but then it will be time for me to show you mine."

His words chilled yet enthralled her. He gripped her hand a little tighter, and she rubbed her thighs together without realizing it.

"I want you to experience the euphoria that comes with killing with your own two hands," Bryan said, his eyes going dark and seductive. "No poisons, no medical malpractice. Just good old-fashioned murder."

Shelby quivered. A sweet heat moved through her like delirium, and she sucked in her bottom lip as visions of brutal violence danced across her mind. She doubted she could do it on her own, but with the guiding hand of an infamous serial killer, she might find success and an even greater thrill of killing than before. All she needed was confidence. With

Bryan by her side she'd have encouragement. His wealth of experience would enrich her. He might just prove to be the best friend she'd ever had.

"Okay, *my Bryan*," she said with a coy smile. "Let the games begin—and let nothing stand in our way."

CHAPTER FOURTEEN

SHELBY LEANED AGAINST THE WALL. The rumors had set her on edge, but now that she was having them confirmed by her supervisor, her system flooded with angst, her levy of faux normalcy forming hairline fractures.

"You seem rattled," the head nurse said. "Don't be. These things happen sometimes. I'm sure it will blow over."

But Shelby had a different view of the situation. Of all the people she'd murdered, she wouldn't have thought James Pinsent's death would be the one to pose a threat. He'd come to the hospital with a long history of cardiovascular problems. Giving him another heart attack shouldn't have raised any eyebrows. The news that his family had filed a wrongful death suit against the hospital left Shelby trembling, so she put her hands in her pockets to hide it.

"A full investigation will clear this up," the head nurse assured her. "That's why we're talking to everyone who works this wing. We need to account for every treatment he received and every bit of medicine that was used, to prove his heart attack was by natural causes and not malpractice."

Shelby's mouth was so dry it proved difficult to speak. "Have they ordered an autopsy?"

The head nurse narrowed her eyes. "Well, yes, Shelby. I believe that's what opened this whole can of worms in the first place."

Shelby bit her bottom lip. If she asked too many questions it would raise suspicion, but considering this was the first official word she'd received about this whole situation, she hoped basic enquiries wouldn't draw too much attention. Still, she had to be careful choosing her words.

"Did they find something . . . unusual?" she asked.

Her supervisor tilted her head, as if examining Shelby. "I've not been given all the details. I've only been asked to investigate."

At least the police weren't the ones investigating—yet.

"Now," the head nurse said, "I'll need you to write up a report for me detailing your work with Mr. Pinsent. Give as many details as you can. We need to go over *everything* with a fine-tooth comb."

Shelby nodded, already pondering how truthful she should be. Bad ideas swirled as she tried to concoct the right lies to save herself. But would they really help? She didn't doubt the investigation would be thorough. Charts would be read. Medicine closets would be inventoried. Time clocks would be audited. Perhaps deaths that occurred outside of hospice would be investigated to compare the findings. Shelby thought she'd been careful, but one thing she'd learned from her obsession with true crime cases was there was no such thing as the perfect murder.

Her supervisor patted her on the back. "Don't worry. We'll get to the bottom of this."

Bryan coughed over the sink, his throat stinging as if it were full of broken razor blades. His lungs ached and a heavy congestion rattled his chest. When he finally produced something, blood misted the porcelain. The coughing fit over, he drew his handkerchief and dabbed the corners of his mouth, turning the cloth red.

It wasn't the first time he'd coughed up blood—he'd even pissed it when he'd had kidney stones—but this was the most blood to come out of him at one time. He ran the sink to wash it down the drain, wishing to forget about it. Worrying about his health wouldn't improve it, and he hated doctors and hospitals. If he had emphysema or cancer, at least he had a nurse in his life. Not that he would ever tell Shelby. He was already self-conscious about being older than her—particularly given her hatred for the elderly. He knew he wasn't *that* old yet, but his ailing health served as a constant reminder he wasn't too far away.

Finished cleaning up, Bryan returned to the music room to practice the piece he'd been working on. It was coming along nicely and the quality of it excited him. For too long he'd doubted his talent. Now he realized he'd merely lacked a muse. Creating something new had been difficult at first because he was out of practice, but as he'd continued to write the music it began to flow as naturally as if he'd been playing the song his entire life. It was working now because he had someone for it to work *for*. He was motivated again to impress someone else, someone he wanted to please, to entice.

Bryan was thinking this just as he heard Shelby come in the front door. He'd given her a spare key, even though he was almost always home. He just liked her having it. It made her seem like more than an employee, or even a friend. Bryan had begun to think of her as his surrogate family, and often wished she could be more.

The poor girl entered the manor in tears.

Bryan rose from the organ and went to Shelby. Seeing her in any state of distress twisted something in him. The feeling was surprising. He'd been capable of expressing sympathy but had never really felt it before. After the death of Alice Fuller, his ability to empathize had rapidly disintegrated, leaving him a hollow shell of a human being, incapable of feeling for others. It'd been a helpful tool for his other killings, so he'd honed the emotional void, deliberately distancing himself from the rest of his species until he was something else entirely, an aberrant amalgamation of man and beast.

His Shelby was unraveling all of that without even trying. Bryan cared for her deeply and wasn't afraid to feel that. He hated to see her cry. It made him want to hurt people.

"What's wrong, love?" he said, putting his hands on her shoulders and leaning over so his face was level with hers.

She sniffed, her face scrunched and pink. "I'm in trouble, Bryan. Big trouble."

She told him about an investigation at the hospital. Shelby blubbered as she revealed the details, shaking in his grip. Though she was right to be concerned, the urge to comfort her dominated any rational thought Bryan may have had. He embraced her and kissed the top of her head.

"It's alright, my Shelby. Dry those eyes. There's nothing to get so worked up about. Nothing's happened yet."

"But they're on to me."

"Did someone say that?"

"No. I just feel it, you know?"

"That's the paranoia talking. Don't get worked up over something that hasn't happened yet—something that may never happen." He couldn't help but think of his rendezvous with old age, but he dismissed the thought. "So many times I thought the police were about to knock down my door, but they never did."

"This is different. Your murders were all in different places. Mine have always been at the hospital. My timecard punches will show I was on duty when Pinsent and the others died. My clearance code will show how many times I went in and out of the pill closet to swipe medicine."

"They have no reason to suspect you of anything."

He ran his hand up and down her back. She pulled him in tighter and pressed her head against his chest. Bryan breathed deep. He would gladly hold her like this forever.

"I'm just so scared," she said. "What if they put two and two together and . . . and—"

"Listen to me. Now isn't the time to panic, but it is the time to protect yourself. Do you have anything in your apartment to link you to the murders? Any medicines you stole from work or anything like that?"

She shook her head. "No. I bagged them up and tossed them in a dumpster across town."

"Clever girl." He hesitated, then said, "What about the pictures?"

Shelby sucked in air, tears rolling down both cheeks. "I did it . . . I deleted them. It killed me to do it, but you were right. I can only hope they can't pull them up again by searching my digital record with the phone company. God, I'm so fucked."

"You're not," Bryan assured her. "This investigation has only just begun. It's standard procedure when a lawsuit comes up, right?" She nodded, and he went on. "You're far from a suspect. You've no criminal record and have a significant history at the hospital. *If* you become a suspect, you'll know it. There will be signs." The urge to comfort her overwhelmed him, and he blurted out what he'd been thinking since the start. "And if it ever looks like they're coming for you, you won't be all alone. You'll have me, and we'll make our escape—together."

She gave him a curious look and pulled away. "What? No, no. I can't drag you into my mess."

"You said nothing would stand in our way."

"But Bryan—"

"Let's not argue. Again, nothing has happened yet. Stressing about all the bad things that could happen in life never helps matters, and it's no way to live. I get that this is a frightening situation to be in. I understand it in a way other people never could—you know that."

She stared into his eyes. "You were afraid too, weren't you? That's why you quit."

"But I didn't allow myself to live in fear. I merely took precautions, as you are right now. You destroyed all potential evidence. Now you just need to lie low. Keep going to work and doing all the things you would normally do—all except killing, of course. I'm not saying you quit murdering for good, just go on hiatus. Once this all passes, you can switch to a different hospital in some other town, but for now, you need to act like nothing is wrong."

She wiped the tears from her cheeks. "Yeah, I know. You're right. I just . . . I just never had anything like this happen before. It's scary."

"I know, love." He took her hands. "But come what may, we'll get through it—together."

When she smiled up at him with wet eyes, her lips were the color of the roses Alice Fuller had plucked on that day long ago—a day that had changed Bryan's life forever. In Shelby's smile, he saw a universe open to him, one he'd been denied access to for decades, and in that instant he knew there was nothing he wouldn't do for her. He would hide her from police. He'd spend his inheritance and go on the run with her. He would kill with her, and he would kill for her, sparing no expense to ensure she felt his love.

"You're so good to me," Shelby told him.

Though he ached to kiss her lips, he didn't feel it was right in this vulnerable moment, so he planted one on her cheek.

"Nobody's ever been this nice to me," Shelby said. "Why're you so sweet?"

He gave her the only answer he could, the only thing he was sure of anymore.

"Because you're mine."

Bryan really knew how to cheer a girl up. Just being back at the manor with him made Shelby feel a hundred times more secure than she had while scrambling through her apartment alone, looking for pill bottles, syringes, and rat poisons to dispose of. Though the threat of being discovered still loomed, in Bryan's embrace it didn't loom so large. It wasn't just that he was a man or that he was older. There simply was comfort in companionship and power in friendship. Their personal bond had developed quickly but richly, for they were two lost souls finding a subtle salvation in each other. All those long, lonesome nights were behind her.

Shelby had wanted a Clyde to her Bonnie, but now she felt like she'd found something much more, and that gave her a profound sense of peace, even as the rest of her life was in upheaval.

Perhaps that life was being phased out for a reason. Maybe it was meant to be put behind her, to make room for a whole new chapter in a story of two. It felt good to be contemplating just what her relationship with Bryan was rather than stressing about what was going on at work. It felt *right*.

But what was this thing between them? It wasn't quite a romantic relationship, and yet she felt like she was falling in love with him. Did he fulfill some need that had germinated out of her problems with her family—her *daddy issues*? Was his friendship so valuable to her because she lacked other real friends, or because he could know her in a way no one else ever could? There were many different types of love—just as there were many different types of killers—and as with motivations for murder, there was constant overlap between the forms of love. She wouldn't be able to classify this on her own. It was something she and Bryan would have to figure out together.

She hoped they'd be doing a lot of things together.

As for now, they headed to Beatrice's bedroom. It was just the thing to lift Shelby's spirits, and Bryan knew it. Somehow, already, he knew her so well.

Because you're mine, she thought.

The phrase delighted her. Had anyone else said this, it would have felt either threatening or silly, but coming from Bryan's lips the sentiment was reassuring, a verbal embrace.

They entered the bedroom loudly, to startle their victim. Beatrice jolted and drew her blanket over her like a child trying to ward off the boogeyman.

"No!" she shouted. "Get out!"

Shelby laughed, the stress of the day leaving her as she opened her medical bag. Though she'd tossed out many tools of the trade to avoid incriminating herself, she'd put her newly purchased instruments into the bag before coming over. She'd bought them for this very occasion and wasn't about to let them go to waste.

Bryan's father had been right. Life went by fast. You had to enjoy it while you could.

She drew the items from the bag and placed them atop the dresser, where Bryan could see them but his mother couldn't. The old woman was now completely bedridden thanks to Shelby's medical treatments, but her pain was far from over. Bedsores covered her body, her limbs bloated from worsening diabetes, and as Bryan examined Shelby's new tools, Beatrice mumbled pleas for mercy. They ignored her.

Shelby pointed at the first item on the dresser. "Drain cleaner."

Bryan smacked his lips and nodded.

Shelby pointed to the next item. "Caulking gun."

Bryan chuckled and motioned to the third item. "And these?"

She picked up the plastic container. "They're sewing needles."

"Are we sewing something up?" he whispered. "My God, you really are Dr. Frankenstein."

She batted his arm playfully. "You'll see what they're for."

"You know . . . I have a surprise too." He reached into his blazer and withdrew a spindle of tightly wound metallic string. "Piano wire. We got rid of the grand piano years ago, but I still have plenty of this stuff in the music room." His voice fell to a whisper again. "Maybe with this she won't be able to squirm so much."

Shelby beamed. Then her expression grew serious, sympathetic. "Are you sure you want to do all this? I know you were hesitant before."

"Yes," he admitted with a long exhale. "And in a way, I still am hesitant. But in a much bigger way, I want to see this through. Not because of all that's happened between Mom and me, but because of what is happening now between you and me."

Touched by this, Shelby kissed his cheek. He'd kissed her before, but this was the first time she'd planted her lips on him. The awe this brought to his face made Shelby turn pink. She felt suddenly like a schoolgirl crushing on a teacher, and the notion only made her tingle more.

Beatrice groaned from her resting place. "Hospital . . . please . . . call an ambulance."

"Not to worry," Bryan told her. "We're going to fix you right up." He winked at Shelby. "We're gonna fix you *real good*, Mommy dearest."

The treatment began.

Shelby guided Bryan through each step and handled the parts he was too nervous to do himself. It was a team effort, after all, and she delighted in teaching him. She already felt she'd learned so much from Bryan. It felt good to give something back.

With Beatrice's wrists bound in piano wire, not only was she unable to fight, but the tightness of the wire risked permanent damage to the nerves in her hands. What pleased Shelby most about this was that Bryan had bound the old woman himself, even as she'd screamed his name with tears rolling down her swollen cheeks.

Shelby snickered, knowing the woman's eyes were about to get a lot redder.

Dipping the Q-tip in drain cleaner, Shelby held Beatrice's left eyelid open and swabbed the bloodshot eyeball. The patient shrieked like a swine in a slaughterhouse. The only word she spoke was her son's name—repeatedly, in a high-pitched squeal. Shelby kept checking on Bryan, making sure he could handle this. His smile reassured her, and they started on the other eye, coating it.

The sewing needles came next.

Shelby had only ever fantasized about doing this. If the killings really were at risk of ending, she wanted to go out gloriously, so she drove the first needle under the nail on Beatrice's baby toe. When the patient started kicking, Bryan wrapped her ankles in piano wire too, grinning as he worked up a sweat. Shelby watched on with pride, then handed Bryan a needle. They looked at each other in a silent expression of understanding—one of acceptance, of love.

Shelby grinned. "Do it, my Bryan."

And with her beside him, he could.

Bryan chose the nail on his mother's big toe. His eyes went wide with excitement at the flow of blood, and Shelby relished seeing the killer inside him rise to the surface, the dormant Hooded Devil resurrected to bring his special brand of horror back to this rotten world. He drove the next needle into the sole of his mother's foot, pushing it as deep as it would go into the bloated meat.

The needling continued. The deadly duo peppered the old woman with these tiny daggers. The needles went in her cheeks, nostrils, and septum, driven under her fingernails and through the webbing of flesh between her thumb and index finger. They were forced through fat and pounded deep into tissue, leaving Beatrice Vives a writhing mess of pain. Shelby thought of needling the bitch's nipples but didn't want to expose Bryan to the sight.

Instead, she switched to the caulking gun.

"I've been most curious about that," Bryan admitted. "What are you going to do, fill her big, fat mouth?"

"No. She'll just spit it out or swallow it. My idea was to incapacitate her. The needles make her fingers and toes useless, and the piano wire disables her. The drain cleaner has clouded her vision and could even leave her blind." She held up the caulking gun like a movie gunslinger. "This is to make her deaf."

Bryan's face seemed to fall, and Shelby briefly worried she'd gone too far. But then he looked at her and grinned.

"That's brilliant," he said.

Thrilled to impress him, Shelby wedged the nozzle of the caulk tube into Beatrice's ear canal and squeezed the trigger as her patient screamed for help that would never come.

CHAPTER FIFTEEN

IT WAS ALMOST A SHAME Mom couldn't hear his new toccata. Bryan could even hear it as a concerto, though he lacked the orchestral arrangement to accompany his organ. His mother had often nagged him about wasting his talent, but Bryan doubted she would have nice things to say about him writing his own music again. He only wished she could hear this because he knew it would irk her to find out who he'd composed it for.

Shelby sat on the fainting couch, watching as Bryan stroked the keys in a rich C minor melody. His feet danced upon the pedals. Though the notes were strong, the toccata was ethereal, as if he'd lifted the music out of some haunted chamber. But the true haunted chamber was the one in his heart. It had ached for something for so long, and he'd only filled it with ghosts and fading memories. Now his heart pumped something other than his sour blood. Inspiration flowed through his veins and drove the music from his soul to his fingertips. As he moved toward a swelling Picardy cadence, he caught a quick glimpse of Shelby reflected in the windowpane. He always marveled at her soft, round face, but looking at her now, his breath caught in his chest. Her image was pale white, making her appear angelic, and though he couldn't read her expression, he could feel the warmth radiating from her.

She likes it, he realized with joy. *She really likes it.*

The organ was not for everyone. Like bagpipes, the sound of it was an acquired taste, and though she'd complimented him before, he'd worried someone her age would see the organ as too old-fashioned—corny, even. But when he'd told her he'd written something new, she'd practically begged him to play it for her.

He closed his eyes again, feeling his way through the rest of the piece as he floated in the nebulous sphere of sound. In this sweet moment, he felt like his idols—Bach, Saint-Saëns, Alain, Boëllmann, Franck, Mendelssohn. He was The Phantom of the Opera playing for the beautiful, young soprano, Christine. He wasn't just a sad old man wandering through a silent house. Though he was sick, he was still alive, and there was still joy left to be had.

As he played the final notes, he felt Shelby's presence behind him. She'd risen from the fainting couch and was hovering over his back like a guardian of his gift, and when Bryan finished, she bent over and put her arms around him.

"It's so beautiful," she whispered.

"You really think so?"

"Absolutely. That you have something like that inside you . . . it's just incredible."

He put his hand on her arm and turned his head to see her. "I couldn't have brought it out of myself without you."

"Me?"

"You inspire me. That's why it's dedicated to you."

She hugged him tighter. "Oh, Bryan. That's so sweet. Do you have a title?"

"I do." He took her hand and kissed it. "I call it 'Because You're Mine.'"

Shelby came around the bench and sat beside him. They gazed into each other's eyes, but neither of them found the right words, so Shelby only rested her head on his shoulder. They joined hands, interlocking their fingers, and stared out the window at the rust of the treetops against the backdrop of a tombstone sky.

"This was a wonderful present," Shelby finally said.

"Consider it an early birthday gift."

"Well, then, I think it's time for me to give you a present in return."

"Having you in my life is all the present I need."

She released a soft sound of happiness on her breath. "Same. But while you've been working on your masterpiece, I've been working on mine."

He looked at her curiously, though he knew exactly to what she was referring.

"Mother," he said.

Shelby nodded. "I think it's time for the grand finale."

A sweet chill erected the hairs on Bryan's neck. "The last movement."

"That crone has been through a lot tonight. I say we let her stew in her misery until tomorrow, and then . . ."

"We drop the curtain," Bryan murmured.

The finality of it hit him like an avalanche. All the years he'd fantasized of being rid of his mother, and now he was facing the reality of her approaching death.

It would also be his first murder in decades. The heaviness of that had come in layers. Revved from meeting another killer, he'd entertained the possibility of donning the red hood once more, and now, with Shelby showing him the joy of poisons, he had the means.

"Heck of a way to kick off my thirties," she said with a smirk. "My first murder as part of a duo—and with an infamous serial killer, no less."

"You flatter me."

"Don't be so modest. You're a big deal. I feel like a fangirl who just got to join her favorite band."

She leaned into him again, and Bryan put his arm around her. He couldn't get enough of the physical touch. He'd been involuntarily cut off from intimate human contact for so long as to be starved of it, and he ate her affection greedily, like an animal that didn't know when its next meal would come.

"Shall I wear the hood when we do it?" he asked.

Shelby's eyes went wide with delight.

"It'd be symbolic for me," Bryan said, "but more than that, it would be a final torture for my mother to find out who I really am, to know she'd raised a killer."

"Oh, Bryan . . ." Shelby said with awe. "I couldn't imagine a better send-off for her than that."

CHAPTER SIXTEEN

THINGS WERE QUIET AROUND MERRIMACK Memorial Hospital. Not the comforting kind of silence, but an eerie stillness that tore at Shelby's nerves. Her fellow employees kept their heads down in their work when Shelby came around, but she thought she heard them whispering when she walked away. The head nurse was nowhere to be found, even though she was on the schedule. Shelby couldn't help but picture her in a small room at a police station, telling detectives about a certain mousy CNA who'd roused her suspicion. It was a paranoid fantasy too close to being a reality. Shelby reminded herself of what Bryan had said about the futility of worrying, but still she remained uneasy throughout the day. She had the powerful urge to hurt someone—just to vent some stress—but she controlled herself and did her job to the best of her ability, being social and polite with patients and trying to appear happy around staff.

That her supervisors did not ask her to work any overtime only added to the tension. Shelby almost never left work on time, and even with the head nurse out, there were other superiors who could have asked her to stay late. Though she was relieved to get out of there, anything out of the ordinary left her apprehensive. As she walked to her car, the autumn wind seemed extra cold, and she hugged herself against the cutting breeze. She turned her head in all directions, looking for any shadow that might creep up on her, half expecting the flash of police sirens.

Once safe in her vehicle, she exited the parking lot and put on a playlist of organ music by classical composers to remind her of Bryan. Just thinking about him made Shelby feel safer. He also made her feel cherished, his arms around her forming an impenetrable force field that warded off all the sadness and pain and anxiety that had plagued her since losing her child. She'd begun feeling uneasy when away from him. He was her calming agent. Without Bryan, Shelby felt vulnerable and exposed, her soul walking naked through the valley of the shadow of death.

She ached for him. She'd gotten so used to being alone, but now she feared it.

My Bryan, she thought as the music played. *You're mine.*

And tonight was their big night.

It was as if they were going on a date, only better. By committing a murder, they were forming a union in blood. She could think of nothing more bonding than two people taking the life of a third. It was the sort of thing that created an unbreakable link, stronger even than marriage or family. There was no divorcing a homicide. Even if she and Bryan grew estranged one day, this would always connect them, an event so intense it could never be forgotten. It would forever couple their hearts in murder—the ultimate in human intimacy.

Before heading to the manor, she decided to swing by her apartment for a quick shower, some fresh makeup, and a change of clothes. She wanted to look and smell good tonight, for everything to be perfect. She'd never dolled herself up for Bryan before. He saw her as beautiful even when she felt dumpy and plain. Shelby wondered how he might react to a pretty dress and a little eyeshadow, and it made her wish she had time to really do her hair, maybe even finally go to a salon and follow it up with a pedicure. Arousing him aroused her, and she found his attention flattering, even alluring. His romanticism had grown on her. She'd had other men in her life who'd made her feel special, but no one had ever written her a song before, and she couldn't imagine ever meeting someone else whom not only understood her need to kill but also related to it. Even though they hadn't had sex or kissed on the lips—and even if they never did—Shelby and Bryan shared a tenderness that went deeper than any other relationship had offered her, and she knew he felt the same. It showed in every sweet word he uttered and every grand gesture he made.

She was smiling as she pulled into the parking lot of her apartment complex. It was the first real smile she'd worn all day, but it was short-lived, for as she drove around the back of her building, Shelby spotted the three patrol cars at the end of the lot, directly under the staircase leading to her apartment.

Her knuckles ran white as she clenched the steering wheel. Breath catching in her lungs, she turned down the alley between the two buildings so not to drive past the police. Did they know what kind of car to look for? Did they have her license plate already? She swallowed hard as she left the complex and pulled back onto the street.

"Oh fuck," she whimpered. "Oh fuck, oh fuck, *oh fuck*."

She headed back the way she'd come, taking the fastest route to Bryan's house, and this time she looked up at the buildings as she passed. The living room window of her apartment faced the street. The lights were on—even though she kept them off when she wasn't home.

Tears filled her eyes. "Oh my God . . ."

Pressing the gas pedal, she warned herself not to panic and get pulled over for speeding. She'd instinctually headed toward Bryan, but now she wondered if that was a terrible idea. What if she was being followed? She would lead the police right to Bryan and his tortured mother, a woman laid out in her own filth, bound with piano wire and her ears packed with caulk.

Shelby reached for her phone, then had another thought. If she called him, someone might listen in. Even if no one had tapped her phone, calling created a record. She didn't want Bryan to be the last person she'd called before the cops nabbed her. It might send trouble his way.

Her next thought made her gasp.

They can track my movements with my phone's GPS.

Though not computer savvy, Shelby knew from her true crime shows how a person's phone pinged, revealing their location. Cops didn't even need to plant a tracking device on a suspect's car anymore because everyone willingly carried one on them. On top of this, the entire country was always under surveillance, with security cameras at every business and most private residences. In the digital age, hunting people down had never been easier.

She was debating what to do with the phone when it started buzzing with an incoming call, startling her. The number was local. She did not recognize it. The phone shook in her hand, a bomb readying to detonate. Shelby rolled down her window and flung the phone into the street, where it snapped into pieces that tumbled toward the gutter. Her car was from 2010, so it had no built-in GPS system. Shelby had no laptop with her or anything else traceable.

She drove on, picking up speed.

Just gotta lay low. Have to hide.

Though she'd reconsidered going to Bryan's place, she was still heading there. Where else could she go? Who else could she turn to? This was her hour of need, and there was only one person she needed, one man she wanted above all others.

Looking in her rearview mirror, she noticed no headlights. If the police were behind her, they probably would have just pulled her over—especially if they'd obtained a search warrant on her apartment. Did they need one? Would the landlord legally be allowed to just let the police in without it?

Shelby had told no one about her side job at the manor. She didn't want people at work knowing her personal business and especially didn't want her supervisors to think she was poaching patients from Merrimack Memorial. Estranged from her parents, and having lost touch with girlfriends who'd married and were busy starting families, Shelby didn't have anyone to share stories from her life with. Now that had proved to be a blessing in disguise. If no one knew about her and Bryan, she might be safe with him for a little while—at least until investigators pulled her phone records and identified his number. But even then, there were plenty of places in the mansion to hide, and she and Bryan could figure out a story that would dismiss the calls as being business related without revealing she'd been his mother's private nurse. They could say he'd merely been consulting with her after his mother's release from the hospital. Something along those lines.

They would figure it out. Bryan would be more levelheaded than she could be right now. Too freaked out to think clearly, Shelby needed him more than ever.

"I want only my Bryan," she begged of the universe.

CHAPTER SEVENTEEN

"YOU DID THE RIGHT THING coming to me," Bryan told her.

Shelby seemed racked with guilt over racing to his home, but he wouldn't have wanted her anywhere else. The risk to him didn't matter as much as comforting her did, and he told her so as he wrapped her in his arms.

Shelby sniffed back tears. "Oh, Bryan . . . what am I gonna do?"

"You mean, what are *we* going to do. We're a team, remember?"

"But I don't want to put you in danger."

"You're not, love. The police have no reason to suspect me of anything, and no cause to search these premises. We've hidden your car in the garage, and now we'll hide you here until we're ready to go."

She looked up at him. "Go? Go where?"

"I was thinking," he began. "Why don't we travel? I've all the money in the world. We can go anywhere you want."

"But they'll be looking for me."

"All the more reason to flee."

She blushed. "I've never been anywhere before . . . never even left New England."

"You'll be thirty tomorrow morning. What a perfect time for you to go out and see the world. We'll make it a birthday unlike any other."

She grinned, and Bryan knew in that moment he would kiss her tears away for a lifetime, that he would give the very blood in his veins if it meant his Shelby would smile.

"Look," he said. "We can hide out here or we can see the world. Lady's choice."

"I suppose I could change my hair and appearance. You know, I've always wanted to see Paris . . . but if they're looking for me, they'll track me through plane ticket purchases. Hell, I don't even have a passport."

"Then we'll hit the open road and see all that America has to offer."

She furrowed her brow in contemplation. "All my stuff is at my apartment."

"I'll buy you new things."

"Bryan," she said, giggling despite it all. "You're not my sugar daddy, you're my . . ."

She trailed off, unable—or unwilling—to define their relationship. Bryan waited with bated breath. His heartbeat accelerated. He wanted to hear it from her own lips, but seeing her struggle, he saved her from having to say anything at all.

"It's alright, love," he said, planting a kiss on her forehead. "Everything's going to be alright. You'll see."

It was more than just words of comfort. Bryan believed things would work out in their favor. He had to believe it, for both of them. Otherwise they would disintegrate. Maybe Shelby was right to think the police had found her out, or maybe she was just being understandably paranoid. If she was right and their time together really was limited, he thought they should enjoy it to its fullest while she was still a free woman. And if she was wrong somehow, as he hoped she was, a road trip was still an excellent idea, because Shelby was only going to turn thirty once. Bryan aimed to make her birthday bright and continue that illumination for as long as she would have him . . . or as long as he would last.

"Are you really sure you want to stick with me during all of this?" she asked.

"I've never been more certain of anything."

His Shelby was *all*. Nothing else mattered.

"Okay," she said, taking his hands. "But first things first."

Beatrice was ready to die.

If she'd been able to speak, she might have even begged them to take her life, but Shelby had used the sewing kit to stitch the woman's mouth shut. It was better than listening to her bitch and moan through her last night on Earth. Shelby didn't want the moment ruined. This was for her and Bryan, and it was as important to her as a wedding proposal or pregnancy announcement would be to a normal woman. No bloody pulp of an old hag was going to spoil this.

Shelby also refused to let her fear of being apprehended ruin this night. If her time with Bryan was doomed to end, she wanted to savor every second by his side. So far, she'd done all she could to avoid capture. All they could do now was wait and see how things developed. They would just have to find a balance between enjoying their lives and playing things safe.

She'd be damned if Bryan would not get his present.

A heavy dose of potassium should be enough to widen Beatrice's heart patterns and finish her off. Shelby had some vials left over in her medicine bag, along with the epinephrine she would add, like a chef pinching spices over a bubbling pot of stew. If these didn't kill Beatrice, Shelby would inject her with a ridiculously large dose of insulin. That would put an end to the wicked witch.

As she prepared the shot, Bryan stood at the foot of his mother's bed, smiling down at her. Though they'd been dabbing her eyes with drain cleaner, she responded to movement, so she wasn't completely blind yet. In Bryan's hands was the hood, folded over like a hand towel. Shelby wondered why he'd yet to put it on. Was he having second thoughts about showing his mother he was The Hooded Devil? Was he having second thoughts about killing her?

"You okay?" Shelby asked.

Bryan's eyes sparkled in the soft light of the room. "I want to show you something."

He lured her to where he stood. Bryan nodded toward his mother, who was on her back in a bed of filth. Blood and urine stains had turned the bedsheets from white to a repulsive tie-dye. Still bound in piano wire, her feet and hands had turned purple from lack of circulation. Tiny holes spotted her body, while some of the sewing needles were burrowed too deep to be removed. Beatrice was bloated and jaundiced, sick beyond measure.

Shelby smiled, proud of her work and prouder to have taught Bryan her methods.

"What is it?" she asked him at the foot of the bed.

"Look at this miserable hag," he said, pointing at his mother. "Even in this dire state, I feel no sympathy for her, and no guilt."

"She brought it upon herself, given how she always treated you."

"And how she treated you, too."

"That's nothing compared to a lifetime of abusive parenting."

Bryan rubbed his chin. "You know . . . as much as I've always hated her, I never really thought what she did to me was *abuse* until now. You've helped me see that, Shelby. You've helped me see that love does not have to come with such suffering, even if it does perpetually move toward its own extinction."

Her eyes fell. Though the tenderness was exquisite, there remained in Bryan a focus on inevitable doom. She wanted to ask him about it, but he went on.

"My killings were always a fusion of love and destruction," he said. "The Hooded Devil of yesterday wanted to show the world that all good things end badly. But that was then, and this is now. Things change—sometimes drastically. Perhaps the second coming of The Hooded Devil could be that same expression in a different form."

His eyes met hers, and she saw in them an infinite blue heaven.

"By killing together, as one, we become both sides of the coin—you are the love, and I am the destruction. As a nurse, you are an angel of death—a killer in the guise of caregiver. Therein lies the love. As The Hooded Devil, I was ferocious brutality. I was chaos. Therein lies the destruction."

Though Shelby appreciated the poetry of his sentiment, she was a little confused.

"I don't understand," she admitted. "What is it you want to show me?"

He unfolded the hood. The crude face looked up at her. Though he hadn't changed it, the demon mask seemed somehow more nightmarish than before. The true dread was in the knowing. This wasn't a Halloween costume. This was the fashion of death, as macabre as a hangman's black hood or the uniform of a concentration camp Nazi. Someone had worn it only in the act of ripping the life away from fellow human beings.

"You've shown me your way," Bryan said. "Now I must show you mine."

He placed the hood in her hands.

Shelby's eyes went wide. "Bryan . . . I . . . I—"

"It's time, my Shelby." He pointed at his mother. "Your killing her is your gift to me. My gift to you is showing you how good it feels to be brutal, to unleash all your anger and despair on a living victim. It is the greatest way to vent, and you need to vent now more than ever. Free yourself of your worries, love. Rid yourself of your troubles by transferring your suffering onto another. I promise you—killing with your own two hands is the best this life offers us. Nothing has ever come close to giving me that same feeling of euphoria." He gave her a bashful grin. "Well, nothing until you came into my life."

Staring into the face of The Hooded Devil in her hands, Shelby gripped the material tight. She was speechless.

Bryan whispered in her ear, making every fine hair on her body rise.

"Let The Hooded Devil be reborn," he said.

Taking the deepest breath, Shelby put the hood over her head.

Inside, it smelled of old sweat and dried blood. She found the aroma intoxicating. The cloth was soft against her cheeks, making her think of fresh linen on a clothesline during a warm spring day. Peering through the eyeholes, Shelby felt like a movie villain, like she was about to rob a bank or slaughter teenagers at a summer camp. But most of all she felt powerful, something she'd never felt before. The hood gave her excitement, but it was Bryan who had given her this confidence, and for that she would repay him with as much spilt blood as he desired. For her Bryan, she would kill hundreds, thousands—men, women, and even children. Kill anyone, any time, any place. She would murder God himself just to see her Bryan's eyes twinkle the way they did right now.

Shelby held the syringe to the light. Liquid death swished within like fine wine. She gushed at Bryan, and he stepped in close behind her, his whole body pressed to hers. His hands went to her hips, mouth grazing her earlobe.

"Show me," he whispered.

He moved his hands to the one she held the syringe with and turned the needle downward, so that Shelby gripped it like a knife.

Bryan whispered once more before stepping away. "Show me your love."

Trembling with a flood of emotion, Shelby stepped to the edge of the bedside. Beatrice stared up at her with bloodshot eyes, but Shelby could read nothing in her expression. The old woman no longer appeared human to her. She was merely a springboard for Shelby's new life with Bryan.

Shelby raised her arm high, the needle releasing a single drop of poison that seemed to fall in slow motion upon Beatrice's nose. The crone moaned—a sound that unleashed thirty years of Shelby's sorrow. She exploded into violence. She stabbed the needle into Beatrice's breast, and before her victim could even react, Shelby pulled the weapon free and stabbed her again, careful not to break the needle while driving it into her fat neck. The syringe rose and fell. Blood left the body in a gruesome ejaculation. Beatrice writhed, causing the headboard to pound the wall, knocking pictures from their hooks. A framed photo of Beatrice holding baby Bryan shattered as it hit the nightstand.

Shelby continued stabbing.

Inside the mask, her breath came back at her, moistening her flesh. Her heart shuddered. It felt as if her blood were burning her veins, and yet she couldn't help but laugh with joy.

Bryan was right.

This was right.

She felt his hands on her shoulders, back, and finally, her hips. And as she stabbed Bryan's mother to death, Shelby grinded back into him with her buttocks, and when he unbuttoned her jeans, Shelby reached back over her shoulder with her free hand and ran her bloody fingers through his hair. With the other hand, she kept stabbing, even as their lovemaking began.

CHAPTER EIGHTEEN

STEPPING DOWN FROM THE WINNEBAGO, Bryan stretched in the gray light of dawn as the sun slowly rose over the Arizona desert. The colors of the rock formations were rich even in the dimness, but by noon they would be a lush rainbow of reds. Shelby had made a good call stopping at this RV park. Rather than drive through the night, they could enjoy the view as they continued to California. Shelby had never seen the Pacific Ocean. They were going to fix that.

They'd been experiencing a lot of new things together.

After burying Mom's corpse under her favorite tree—right beside the skeletal remains of Alice Fuller—Bryan and Shelby had begun planning. They'd mapped out all the places they wanted to see but, by going at their leisure, they allowed themselves plenty of opportunities for detours and spontaneous adventure. With November having struck the northeast with frigid temperatures, the duo headed west, following the sunsets to warmer climates with big skies and sandy shores. Along the way, they shamelessly indulged themselves, practicing first on a Caucasian hitchhiker and then on a homeless Native American. Bryan gave the hitchhiker a lethal dose of insulin, telling the young man it was heroin. Shelby graduated to an actual knife for her next stabbing, planting the blade in the hobo's chest and puncturing his lung. While these murders had given them a rush, they knew they were only rehearsals for the grand tour that lay ahead.

Bryan still wasn't feeling well, but he was feeling better. Despite his health problems, the company of a younger woman had invigorated him. The aches of his body no longer held him back from living life. Time was promised to no one. Death could take him, just as the police could take Shelby. With the world ready to end any day, there was nothing to life but this very moment.

Shelby came down the steps of the RV and joined Bryan as he gazed upon the Painted Desert. She snaked her arms around his waist.

"I didn't think you were awake," he said.

"You know I hate sleeping without you. Jeez, it's cold out here in the mornings."

"Sorry, I just like to watch the sun come up," he said. "The light used to hurt my eyes. I'm not sure what happened, but now I don't mind it so much."

"Things change," she said. She tickled his ribs. "Come back inside."

"Oh, alright."

As they climbed into the luxury road vehicle, Bryan smelled the coffee Shelby had put on. She knew how he liked to sip while reading the morning news. Pouring himself a mug, he sat beside her on the sofa, and she tucked her feet under his butt to warm her toes. He gazed upon her with wonder, endlessly amazed to have her. Shelby rested her head and closed her eyes. She refused to take part in anything this early. Bryan smiled as he took his first sip of coffee, put his laptop on the table, and opened the browser.

He'd never cared about world news. He considered himself too deracinated from society to be interested in its endless tragedies and injustices. The only time he'd followed the news was when he'd been an active serial killer, searching the papers for articles about himself. Now he had a similar interest. But instead of looking out for himself, he was looking out for the woman he loved. He'd been checking the local news every morning since they'd fled, looking for any mention of Shelby Brandt without searching her by name, which he worried might be suspicious if the police ever got ahold of them.

Shelby had not called out of work or stopped off at her apartment. She said she didn't expect to return to either place ever again. They'd simply hit the road after putting Bryan's mother in the ground. Bryan rented the Winnebago, lying to the clerks about where he was going, and once they were out of state, he and Shelby went on a shopping spree, giving his girl a whole new wardrobe. Mom had harbored many conspiracy theories about banks and kept thousands in cash inside the wall safe. They'd been using it now, so not to leave a credit card trail.

As he scrolled through the New England news sites, Bryan nearly spit out his coffee when he saw Shelby's face appear on the screen. He read the headline with bated breath.

SEARCH CONTINUES FOR MISSING NURSE

Bryan bit his thumbnail as he read on. This was it. He skimmed to get the important parts.

> *Shelby Brandt was reported missing early last week, just before her thirtieth birthday. Her supervisors at Merrimack Memorial Hospital first suspected something was wrong when Brandt, known for her perfect attendance, did not arrive for her shift . . .*

Bryan skimmed on, looking for anything regarding the investigation into the death of James Pinsent. He saw nothing. There were quotes from Shelby's coworkers describing her as hardworking and liked by staff.

"What the . . . ?" he muttered.

> *Police are concerned because Brandt was last seen leaving the hospital on the same night as a series of burglaries that occurred at her apartment complex in Glenn Cove. Two suspects apprehended later that evening are accused of breaking into Brandt's apartment, as well as three other apartments in the complex. While both men have long criminal records for burglary and robbery, neither has a history of violence, but concern remains regarding Brandt's sudden disappearance.*

"Holy shit," Bryan said, grinning widely.

> *On the evening in question, police got Brandt's cell phone number from her landlord, but the call wasn't*

answered. Records show the phone hasn't been used since . . .

Bryan erupted with the laughter of relief.

> *. . . still being considered a missing person case. "We're just concerned for Ms. Brandt's safety," Police Chief Darryl Hayes stated. "We encourage anyone with any information about her whereabouts to contact us."*
>
> *Dr. Chris Santoni, a coworker of Brandt's, had this to say: "Shelby is a sweet girl and a fantastic nurse. We're all holding out faith she'll return to us safely."*
>
> *If you have any information about Ms. Brandt's . . .*

Bryan laughed louder, rousing Shelby.

"Babe?" she asked, groggy.

"Wake up, love," he said, patting her thigh. "You will not believe this."

❦

Bryan had told her everything would be okay, and time had proven him right. Now Shelby had learned to trust him in a way she'd not trusted another person since her parents had betrayed her.

No one was after her. No one suspected her of any wrongdoing. She'd mistaken the police response to a burglary at her apartment with them closing in on her for murder. Thinking back on how she'd panicked, Shelby had to laugh. The unknown call she'd received while fleeing must have been the police trying to contact her to tell her about the break-in.

If the hospital's investigation into the death of James Pinsent had gone anywhere, it had not led to Shelby Brandt.

But now she had a new problem.

"It's gonna look like I ran because of the audit on the hospital," Shelby said. "I've basically incriminated myself by fleeing."

Bryan shrugged as they drove on. "Not necessarily. Your home was broken into. You could say you ran because you feared for your life."

"With all that's going on at the hospital, I'm surprised they haven't issued a warrant for my arrest."

Bryan shook his head. "I doubt they would. The death of that patient would be a civil suit, so it's not exactly criminal. They have no reason to suspect foul play, only medical negligence, right?"

"But it could *become* a criminal case."

"You know you can't live your life stressing about what might happen."

"But how am I going to explain my disappearance?" she asked as they passed another sign announcing the miles left to California.

"You act as if you owe them an explanation," Bryan said.

"Well, don't I?"

"What for? You said you were never going back there, so why bother? Why would you need to explain yourself to people you're never going to see again?"

She played with her hair as she considered this. "So . . . is this our life now? We're going to live in this Winnebago forever?"

"Of course not. I figure we spend a week or two in California, enjoy the beaches and boardwalks, and then we book that trip to Paris."

Shelby gushed. "Oh my God . . . are you serious?"

"Absolutely. Now that we know you're not wanted for any crime, we can get you that passport and go wherever we want—starting with the City of Lights."

She didn't know what to say, but when she was with Bryan, sometimes she didn't have to, for he already knew what she felt.

He took her hand. "It's probably in our best interest for you to talk to the police though, to tell them you're okay."

"And maybe call work to tell them I'm quitting, just for the sake of appearances. We've all been short-staffed and overworked. Stressed to the max. I can just tell them I've had it."

"You're a free woman and can do as you please."

Shelby thought of her job and her apartment and her complete lack of a social life. It would be easy to leave it all behind, particularly because she'd already come to terms with that when she'd believed she was on the run from the law. But now she had the choice to return to her old life or to continue with the new one she'd forged with Bryan.

It was the easiest decision she could make.

As they crossed the border, she squeezed his hand three times. The sun was going down, and the sky was a sea of flame. Shelby put her feet up on the dashboard, her toenails shining with pink polish from her recent pedicure. She had the time to treat herself now. Why put a limit on freedom?

"We should find a couple tonight," she said.

Bryan nodded. "What a lovely idea."

Bryan had always preferred killing the young, and Shelby was young enough to lure them in. She'd always preferred killing old people, and with Bryan by her side, elderly couples were less suspicious of her when she made conversation at diners and tourist attractions. She'd taught Bryan the pleasures of poison, and he'd taught her the ecstasy of frenzy. Together, they were a highly effective predator.

"And what of love?" she asked him.

"What do you mean?"

"Love is what you always destroyed." She hated to ask but had to. "Will you come to want to destroy *our* love?"

He shook his head. "I told you—things change. Our dynamic is different. And what about you? You always killed old farts. What happens when I get old and sick?"

"I could never see you as old," she said, and meant it. "Age is something that happens to people I don't care about. To me, you're ageless."

"And sickness? What about that?"

"Whatever we face, we do it together. You taught me that." She leaned forward. "Speaking of faces . . ."

Shelby popped the glovebox and withdrew what she'd been working on. The pillowcase was purple—her favorite color—and she'd affixed the closed end with short pieces of deer antlers from a pet store, the kind dogs chewed. Using magic marker, she'd created a face more feminine than that of The Hooded Devil, so her mask was akin to his while still being her own creation. To make the eye holes, she'd used the same knife she'd used to kill the homeless man, cutting the pillowcase while the blood was still wet. This gave the mask the appearance of crying blood.

Wearing black lipstick, Shelby kissed the death mask, giving it its own pair of dark lips. She held the mask up before her, satisfied it was complete. She put it on and turned to Bryan, delighting in seeing him smile.

"You know why I love you, my Bryan?" she asked.

He smiled wider. "Why?"

She leaned toward him, panting under the hood. "Because you're mine."

The Winnebago rolled on, following a blood sunset to new horizons.

ACKNOWLEDGMENTS

Thanks and love to Chandra Claypool, Mona Kabbani, Gregg Kirby, Aron Beauregard, Scott Cole, Bryan Ferry, Bear, and Shadow. Additional thanks to Edward Lee, C.V. Hunt, Brian Keene, Wrath James White, Shane McKenzie, Bryan Smith, Daniel J. Volpe, and Jack Ketchum.

Big thanks to all my readers and fans around the world.

Special thanks to Tom Mumme—always.

KRISTOPHER TRIANA is the Splatterpunk Award-winning author of *Gone to See the River Man*, *The Old Lady*, *Full Brutal*, *They All Died Screaming*, and many other terrifying books. His work has been published in multiple languages and has appeared in many anthologies, drawing praise from *Rue Morgue Magazine*, *Cemetery Dance*, *Scream Magazine*, and many more. He is also a regular columnist for the magazines *Backwoods Survival Guide* and *Prepper Survival Guide*.

He lives in New England.

Get signed books at: TRIANAHORROR.COM

Visit him at: Kristophertriana.com and on Substack, Instagram, Facebook, and TikTok.

Printed in Great Britain
by Amazon

50053351R00098